Lean On Me

Marybeth Velez

Contents

Part 1

Mateo

I sip hot coffee at my usual seat in the far back corner of the shop. I've been coming in here for the last two weeks, ever since leaving the hospital to try and recover more independently. I still have to go there everyday for physical therapy, but at least the rest of my day can be spent outside those sterile walls and away from the constant reminder that war is ugly. I scratch at the few days of scruff on my chin and watch as the door to the coffee shop swings open, ringing the bell to notify the staff of a customer.

A young woman enters, her auburn hair pulled back into a ponytail and a smile on her beautiful face. She's listening to music in her own little world, evident by the thin white wires running along her cheeks and down her shirt to where they connect to her phone. I know it's not a phone call because her lips are moving, silently singing along as her hips sway to the beat. My own lips curl and I realize it's been a while since I've genuinely smiled at someone. Her eyes meet mine and she stops singing, her cheeks turning a light shade of pink with embarrassment.

"Don't stop on my account," I say as she stands next to my table at the end of the long line. Being this close to a hospital means a constant flow of customers for the shop. Every doctor and nurse in the area drops in to grab their morning Joe and they're most likely back by 10am for another pick-me-up.

"Sometimes I forget where I am," she laughs softly. I hate to admit it, but I love the sound immediately.

Always the joker I remind her sarcastically, "Busy coffee shop. Long line. Lots of people." I look around as if to show just how many of us there are.

She covers her face with a hand and shakes her head. "Thanks for making this whole experience less awkward." Now it's my turn to chuckle at her sarcasm. I hold up my coffee in salute and she turns back to the line. I try not to stare at her ass, but it's so nicely wrapped in a tight pair of jeans and it's been long time since I've been with anyone. She's tall, probably only a little shorter than my six feet, and has a knock out body. Small waist, but not in the skinny super model way, more like a woman who takes care of her body and enjoys working out.

I can appreciate a body that's well taken care of. Fitness used to be my thing. I started every morning with a jog, lifted weights in the evening and swam laps whenever possible. I run my hand along my thigh, feeling the way the skin dips and the tightness that comes with a heavy dose of scarring. When she turns around again, smiling at me,

I relax my hand so I don't draw attention to the achy limb. I've missed this. The way it feels to flirt with a girl and the anticipation of more.

I have my face in a book, but I haven't been reading. I keep looking up to where she waits, watching as she plays with her hair and laughs with the other customers. After getting her drink she makes her way by my table. I notice her slowing down, almost as if she's waiting for me to ask her something. I flip another page in the book and pretend not to notice her nearness. The old Mateo would ask for her number, maybe even skip that step and go straight for a date invitation. But this new Mateo--he's broken. How can I ever expect a woman to want to get naked with me when I can't even stand to look at myself? I've been waiting for the steam to fill the bathroom before I shower and I refuse to wear anything that might put my injury on display.

The pretty stranger moves another step closer and my heart rate picks up. I want her to leave. I don't want to have to be mean or act like an asshole to push her away, but I will if she makes me. Just when I think she's going to say something, the door swings open and a young doctor that I recognize from the hospital steps through. The girl looks up at him and waves, "Good morning Dr. Lowe," she greets and he grins.

"Morning Ashlyn." I feel my jaw tighten at their familiarity. Of course she's into him; he's got everything. He has a career, an un-marred body, and enough confidence that it's obvious even from where I'm sitting. I feel the bile rise in my throat and I hate everything about today already. I check my watch and see that my appointment is in ten minutes and now I'm even more pissed because I know there's no way I'm going to make it if they talk any longer. I refuse to stand up until she's gone. Maybe I'm a coward, but I don't want to taint the picture of her in my mind with the image I'll see when she watches me limp out of here. If I've learned anything from this experience it's that I fucking hate pity.

I'm relieved when she just waves with her fingers and sticks her ear buds back in. She pushes open the door and I watch her through the window look both ways before stepping out to cross the street. When I'm sure she's far enough away, I push myself up on my unsteady leg and wince as I put my weight on it. I'm so fucking tired of being far from the man that I used to be. With a hiss of breath between my teeth and a pinch of my face, I limp slowly out of the shop and head for physical therapy—my only hope at ever getting my life back.

Part 2

A shlyn
 I clip my hospital badge onto my shirt and set my purse and phone inside one of the small lockers. My mind can't stop thinking about the man from the coffee shop and I wonder if I'll ever see him there again. There was something haunting about his eyes and the rescuer in me wanted to reach out. Around here, there are a lot of veterans lost after coming home and it's usually difficult for them to find their footing now that they're back. I hope for him that's not the case.

I'm not usually attracted to men that aren't wearing business suits with looks of determination on their face. My last three dates have been with different doctors at this hospital, but I'm always left disappointed when there isn't much passion beneath the clean cut exterior. There was just something about the coffee shop customer that has my interest peeked.

I meet my client just inside the door of physical therapy. He's in a wheel chair without his prosthetic leg because we're only set up to work on his upper body today.

""Hey Levi. How was your weekend?" I point over to the first machine we will be using. I don't dare take the handles of his wheel chair. Around here, patients get pretty upset when you treat them incapable when it comes to a task they've already conquered. I'm usually not in this early on Mondays, but one of the other therapists is taking her maternity leave and we are all helping out with her shifts.

"One party after another," he answers sarcastically. We both know he's still a patient in the hospital until his next surgery is complete. I chuckle at his words and help set up the machine.

"Ok, party animal. Three sets of fifteen. I'm here if you need me." I watch as he begins his set. The door opens and I turn my head to see who's coming it. It's the man from the shop. He's much taller than I thought from the way he'd been slouched behind that table. He's at least six feet tall, longer brown hair than most of my patients, and with a few days of scruff darkening his jaw. He's very muscular; with a broad back and strong arms. I let my gaze fall lower and I find his legs as equally fit—at least from what I can see thanks to the old sweatpants that cover his limbs.

The therapist in me wonders what he's here for, but the question is quickly answered when he starts walking toward the other therapist in the room. He favors his right leg, putting more weight on his left. His limp is noticeable, but it looks like he's on track to getting its full use back. Watching him makes me smile. I know how hard it must be to fight back from a devastating injury.

He hasn't seen me yet. That moment comes when his therapist directs him over to a leg machine. His eyes meet mine and his expression changes from determined to unhappy in just a second. They are the color of dark coffee and I can see the disappointment in them from across the room. He doesn't realize he's been rubbing his leg, but with my eyes on him he suddenly conscious of the movement and he stops immediately.

"Three sets of twenty," Jane directs him. "I'll be there in just a second." She goes back to helping her last patient get into his wheelchair safely. She pushes him past me and asks, "Can you keep an eye on Mateo for a minute? I'm just going to help Jim get to his room."

I nod my head but a deep voice booms, "I don't need a babysitter. It's just a fucking leg press Jane." She laughs and rolls her eyes.

"Fine. Don't look at him." It reminds me of something a frustrated mother would say in answer to her toddlers temper tantrum. Mateo pays us no attention. He's already settled on the machine and adjusting the weight. I find myself watching him when my patient takes a rest.

"I'm going to grab some water," Levi says and he begins to push himself towards the fountain. I cross my arms over my chest and wait for him by the next machine. Only I can't relax because Mateo's face is pinched in discomfort as he tries to extend his injured leg. I'm moving before I even really think about it.

"You need to lift your foot up a little higher. Right now you're lifting with a muscle that isn't meant for it. Move your heel up and it will engage your quad." I slide one hand up his thigh and squeeze the muscle that should be working while lifting his heel up higher with my other hand. His hand is on mine fast, pulling it away from his thigh. His angry expression has me lifting my hands in surrender.

"I've got it." The words feel like a bite as he practically growls them. I have two older brothers so I'm very used to men being insulted when I offer to help. He doesn't scare me, but when I realize I didn't hurt him and he's just being an asshole, I cross my arms and glare back at his scornful eyes.

"What you have right now is a bad attitude. What you'll have after three sets of twenty is a muscle strain. If you want to work backwards then you should make sure Jane knows your new treatment plan when she gets back."

His eyes take me in, but he doesn't say a word. I can see his chest rising and falling from his deep breaths. Finally, he lifts his foot up higher and slams the machine as he presses with new strength. Hmm. I guess I do know what I'm talking about. Satisfied that he'll see I'm right, I turn back to Levi and we move on to the next set. I try to get Mateo out of my head and I vow to not look his direction again even though my skin feels alive with an electric energy. That man is trouble...and everything inside me is responding to it. Looks like a challenge might be the excitement I've been craving.

Part 3

Mateo

Fucking great. Of course she's a therapist here. Dammit. I push the weights up again, my quad muscle burning and the sleek shiny skin near my healing wound pulling tight. When I'm done, Jane will help massage out the scar tissue so moving my leg won't be as uncomfortable. I thought being in the sandbox was torture, but having some one kneed tender skin is a lot worse.

I watch her my stranger helping Levi as I continue my set. She laughs at his jokes and leans over him at times to adjust the machines. I shake my head. He has her wrapped around his finger. I know for a fact that fucker can bend over and change the weights himself, he's just enjoying the view as she does it for him. It pisses me off. I'm feeling so frustrated I'm able to add an extra five pounds to the small amount Jane asked me to try. From the awareness beneath my waist it seems that I'm not just mentally frustrated. I'm having trouble keeping my eyes off her ass and the perfect rack she has bound down by some sort of sports bra I'm sure.

I haven't had sex since the week before we deployed. It's been a long fucking time. Probably the longest dry spell since I lost my virginity at fifteen. It's starting to wear on me. I've tried to help myself out, but the depression I've been feeling over this whole fucking nightmare has made me disinterested in previously enjoyed activities. In other words, I don't even want to fuck myself.

She's trying not to look at me. I can tell because she won't turn around in my direction at all. It's obvious to anyone in here, but Levi isn't going to call her on it because her little act of defiance is putting her tits right in his view. I don't blame him one bit. When she leans over to unlock the wheel of his chair, he looks up at me giving the universal, "Look at that," face. Men are assholes—all of us.

I hate this hour of my day. I hate that I need help. I hate that I should've been at Pines' funeral but I was being wheeled into my second surgery the day they put him in the ground. This is not how I thought we would all come home from our deployment. We should be heroes, but instead I'm just a disabled Marine—scratch that—I'm just fucking disabled. Marine Corps offered me a desk job and I took the medical discharge. I don't want to hold anyone back and I'll never be ok with carrying out my service behind a desk. Fuck that.

I close my eyes as the muscles in my bad leg start to twitch and shake. I'm pushing them really hard today and I know I'll pay the price later. Jane keeps reminding me that it' not a race, but she doesn't know that to me it is. I'm racing to get the fuck out of here. I'm racing to get my leg back. I'm racing to finally get my fucking happiness back. And if I'm honest, I'm racing away from the survivor's guilt I have for taking five shots in the leg instead of one to the head like Pines.

I open my eyes and focus on the ceiling for a minute before I have to switch machines. I squeeze my chewed up muscle in the palm of my hand, willing it to get stronger so I can be done with this place. The half numb feeling I get through the damaged skin only reminds me of how delicate the other therapist was when she corrected my position. Her hand felt like a small shock as she gripped my injured thigh and the sensation ran straight up my leg and into my groin. I'd pulled her hand away before any of my self–loathing thoughts could become dirty and directed at her. She seems too nice to be a part of anything my deprived male brain might think up.

It's the longest hour of my day and when Jane finally brings me over to the table to ice my leg, I can't wait to get it over with. Jane's pager beeps and she pulls it out to check the display. She's the head of the physical therapy department and is always getting emergency calls. "Ashlyn," she calls over to the beautiful girl, holding the door open for Levi to wheel out of. "Can you ice Mateo so I can help work up a plan for the new admit?" Ashlyn's eyes fall to mine and I can see that she' not too happy about the request, but she's a professional.

"Sure." She makes her way over to the ice and grabs a few bags. There are other people in the office with us, but it's quiet in this corner. She comes to stand at my side as I lay down flat on the table where Jane left me. She reaches for the top of my sweats, but I hold them up with one hand and shake my head.

"Just put it on top of the pants," I command.

"It won't get your muscles as cold. It's also easer to tape to your skin." Her fingers dip beneath my waistband and I become suddenly paranoid that I'm going to get hard right here on the table in front of this woman and then I'll never be able to come back. Not that they will kick me out, but after a few month of not reacting to anything, I'm going to be pretty fucking humiliated to get excited about the young therapist dishing out her bad attitude eye roll for eye roll, sarcastic remark for sarcastic remark to my own.

"Suit yourself," she says, dropping the ice on top of my thigh a little harder than necessary. I grunt with the pain. My eyes watch her face, her big hazel eyes inspecting my leg for the best position for the ice. Then I let them fall down her neck and over her rack. She's perfect. Maybe not the ditzy blonde type I used to go for, but something about the way she straightens with confidence around me has my body on full alert. She's clearly good at her job and that makes me wonder what else she might be good at.

"Well?" she asks and I get lost for a second watching her plump lips move. When they grow tight and into a thin line, I realize she's talking to me.

"What?" I lean up on my elbows and look down at my leg.

"Does it feel ok?" she asks and I get from her tone it's not the first time she asked me that.

"I'm missing flesh and muscle. It feels just peachy." Her lip tries to lift into a smile at my words but she stomps it down.

"That's all you're missing?" she leans in and whispers sarcastically, making it a point to look around at each of the veterans in here with entire limbs gone. Point received.

"Thanks for the ice," I say, sitting up and sliding off the table. I don't look back when I leave, and she doesn't stop me to say goodbye.

Part 4

M ateo

I don't stay at my favorite table this time. I grab my coffee and get the hell out of there because I don't want to have a run in with Ashlyn. It's bad enough that I couldn't stop thinking about her yesterday, I don't know how I'll get through session ever again if she's there too. I'm leaving the shop with my coffee in one hand and my phone in the other. I've been texting with my buddy Liam about a good time for him and Lucas to come visit. I'm not really up for any visitors so I keep brushing them off.

I swing the door open and a woman who has clearly had too much coffee comes darting in past me, her small fluff of a dog running circles around her feet. The unruly little creature moves right into my path and since I can't really lift my bad leg that well, I stumble over the flea bag and my cup and phone go flying from my hands and mix in a puddle of coffee and shattered iPhone. FUCK ME.

The other downside....other like there are only two...let's rephrase: one of the many downsides to having a bullet-riddled femur is the inability to bend down swiftly and retrieve my belongings. I can't really bend down much at all. I'm staring down at the puddle when two bright pink shoes come into view. They are attached to tan legs—long, toned, tanned legs. And of course those long toned legs are attached to an equally jaw-dropping body. All of which (can you see where this is headed) is topped with a beautiful face with auburn hair pulled back tightly into a ponytail. Ashlyn.

"Bitch," she mutters to the caffeine infused woman's back. Don't worry, she can't possible hear her over the yappy bark of the little mutt as well as the sheer distance between us since she never bothered to even turn around and see what her rude behavior had caused. Ashlyn bends down and retrieves my belongings and as much as I want to tell her to put them down and then go away so that I can retrieve them my damn self, I don't. We both know it would take me a good twenty minutes and a lot of ugly yoga poses before I could get anywhere near them. It takes ten minutes just to tie my fucking shoe on that foot.

"Thanks," I mutter when she hands me back my wet and probably ruined iPhone.

"No problem. You headed to therapy?" She glances across the street as if to confirm that the hospital is still there and I feel my lips lift into a smile.

"Just finished actually." OK, I might have changed my appointment time in the hope that I'd not run into her again. See how well that worked out?

"Home then?" She asks as a follow up.

"Yes. I live just up the street." I motion to a small apartment building where I've rented a one-bedroom place to be close to the hospital. I still can't drive so I'm left walking everywhere I want to go.

"I'm headed that way too." I listen to her words and know exactly what I should say. I should ask to walk with her, but I don't want to hold her up. Clearly she's been out jogging and having to stay by my side would only slow her down and annoy any able-bodied person.

"Well clear a path for me." I motion for her to be on her way, but she just shakes her head.

"Why don't you join me?"

"I don't think so. I'm all run out for the day." I take a step away from her and towards my place.

"If you only work out that hour in the hospital, your recovery is going to take a long time. You should talk to Jane about adding in a few more exercises so you can get more mobility. Next time you can pick up your own stuff." She takes a few big steps to keep up with me. My gait isn't long anymore, but I'm moving quickly.

"Right because being reminded for an hour a day that I won't ever walk normal again is super fun. I should just stretch that out." I'm an asshole.

"You're a dick. Maybe you should ask Jane about your other therapy options. I know a good surgeon that could remove that stick from your ass while we're at it." Her words make me chuckle.

"It's not nice to make fun of someone with disabilities."

"You're not disabled. Well, unless we count your IQ." She shrugs a shoulder and keeps a serious expression on her face."

"Ouch," I say dryly, but inside I'm laughing. She doesn't hold any punches.

"I run this way every Tuesday and Thursday at 11am. That's when I get off my shift. You should meet up with me. I could spot you as you start to jog again." She looks at me with hope in her eyes.

"I'm not a jogger."

"You were."

"How could you possibly know that?" I'm now making sure to keep moving forward. I need to get inside the safety of my apartment before I agree to something crazy like she's proposing.

"Three reasons. The first is that you are sprint-limping right now and aren't even a little out of breath." She holds up one finger and a chuckle rushes from my mouth. Then she holds up the next. I look at it for a brief second and then train my eyes back on the end of this race—my apartment. "Two, I can tell by your calf muscles you used to run." She's proud of herself for that one. It's kind of cute. I don't let on to that though. I just lift a brow as if I'm not entertained. "And three," she says, turning around to walk backward so she can look at me directly in the face, "I saw your chart."

I stop moving for a second. What. The. Fuck. "How did you see my chart?" She smiles and stops moving, resting her hands on her hips.

"I've been assigned to your case." We are just steps from the stairs that lead up to my place. I'm not going to start going up them until she's gone. All thirty-three of them take time. Usually it takes me about ten minutes from the first step until I reach the top. She follows my gaze and looks up at my building. "Home sweet home," she says with a smile. Then she turns around and starts jogging again. I watch her for a moment. She lifts her hand up to wave behind her and shouts, "See you tomorrow cranky!"

Part 5

A shlyn

Jane takes Mateo's file from my stack. "I've been thinking about our new client," she says as she slides his folder back into her daily slot. "I think I need you on the new case. He's rehabbing a knee injury and that's your specialty. I think you can use the new taping technique from the conference last month." She pulls out the clean, new file and sets it in my stack.

"Sure." I agree, but I'm a little disappointed that I'm not going to get to push Mateo. As if thinking his name summoned him, he pushes through the office door and heads over to the treadmill. Most of our clients get the hang of the routine and don't need much supervision after a few weeks. Mateo is one of those clients. I'm a little irritated that Jane hasn't called him on his lack of effort or added more exercises to push him along. I was looking forward to restructuring his treatment plan.

I'm waiting for my third client of the day, looking through a few other files when Mateo gets off the treadmill and makes his way over. "So should I just keep going through with my usual plan or are you going to switch things up?" He sounds irritable like just having to be anywhere near me pisses him off.

"Change of plans. Jane is back on your case." My words are blunt and straight to the point. I can practically feel the grumpiness rolling off of him. I go back to reviewing the file in front of me.

"Why? Did you ask to be removed or something?" He shifts his feet, looking unsure all of a sudden. It's very different from his hard-ass attitude in our previous encounters.

"No." I don't even bother looking up. He still doesn't move.

"So...you won't be working with me?"

I look up at him slowly, "I'm getting slightly concerned you might have a traumatic brain injury." His lips twitch with a smile but he doesn't let it stretch very far across his face.

"I guess my day just got better." He uses a towel to wipe his forehead.

"It must be your luck day." I'm back to pretending to be overly interested in the folder in front of me. Mateo puts me on edge. He has a big presence even though he's insecure right now. It makes me wonder what he might have been like before the injury. Marines always carry themselves with purpose, but there's something about his determination not to let me in that makes me want to break the wall down even more.

"I wouldn't say that," he says under his breath as he heads to the bike. I watch him try to get on it, my body perched at the edge of my chair. I've seen many men struggle with their new limitations, but watching him do it stings my heart. He's just so defeated. He finally gets his foot into the stirrup but then has to stop and massage his thigh for a minute. I look over at Jane, but she's helping another client. It's not unusual that we have more than one client at a time when they are further along in their recovery and don't need constant supervision.

I try to focus on the folder in front of me, but my eyes keep rising up to where Mateo is. If I were him I'd be feeling frustrated too. Jane should be showing him how to set the bike up for what's best for his body and the limited movement he has in that leg. Needless to say, my afternoon is frustrating and thought provoking. I want to help him, but I'm not going to be able to do it within these walls. He is not my patient.

After an hour, Mateo is covered in sweat. He uses the towel again to wipe it from his face, but it does nothing to clear the smoking hot look of a man after physical work from his face. He holds his water bottle up and lets the cold fluid fall into his mouth. I swallow slowly, lost in the erotic image that will definitely be making an appearance in my dreams tonight. I feel my cheeks flush at the thought. He's been visiting me in the dark ever since I first met him. The last two nights have been pretty intense. If only he didn't hate me in real life.

Mateo tucks the bottle into his small bag and makes his way past my desk. He smells purely male, the clean scent of his body wash mixing with the sweat of his exertion. It's sexy as sin and my thoughts float off to a place I only visit at night, when his strong arms are around me and I'm freely touching each hard plane of his chest. I squeeze my legs together and scold myself for the inappropriate thoughts, but it's been a long time since I got that far with someone. I'm not the kind of girl that sleeps around and since I've been here, none of my dates have made it past date number two.

"Ashlyn," a deep male voice calls and my head snaps up in the direction of the door. "I'll see you tomorrow." Mateo doesn't smile when he says it. I get the feeling I should feel honored to have him say anything to me at all. I haven't heard him talking to anyone at all today and that's not typical for a place full of men used to being a part of a team. I nod my head in answer and watch as he pushes open the door and walks out of my day...but certainly not out of my thoughts.

Part 6

Mateo

I'm up and ready to do something new today. Yesterday I went to therapy ready to get an hour of mental sparring with the girl I can't get out of my head. Instead I found out that she wouldn't be my therapist. That's disappointing in the sense that I've seen her work with other patients and I know she's more of a ball buster than Jane. I've been thinking that maybe I need that. On the other hand, at least my dirty thoughts about her won't cross the patient/therapist boundary. I can imagine bending her over any surface I want without feeling like a complete pervert.

Things are also looking up a little in the sexual release area. The thoughts about Ashlyn flooding my head have seemed to wake up my dick again. It went from declining every invite to join the party to rising to the occasion at the drop of a hat when I think of her or watch her bending over to change the weight on a machine or twist her hair up as she looks over her files. Oh yea, I'm filling up my brain with many images of her hot body and biting lips that can deliver a sarcastic comment better than any other girl I've met.

I tie my first running shoe in no time flat. It's the second one that takes some maneuvering. The bullets to my femur alone would have severely limited my movement given the way they tore through muscle and ripped the connective tissue separating muscle from bone. Only those bullets had nothing on the one that shattered my kneecap. I'm now the proud owner of a titanium kneecap, and the scar tissue and trauma of the extensive clean up the surgeon had to perform. That really fucked me up.

I wince but push through, bending my leg so that I can reach the laces. My forehead is covered in sweat and I'm chewing Vicodin like it's cereal just minutes before I need to be down the front steps to meet up with Ashlyn. It's time to make a bigger effort at getting my life back. I guess I didn't see the rush to do so until there was a girl that got me thinking about the benefits of being able to move the way I used to. And thinking about Ashlyn naked makes me want to move that way again.

I start the slow hobble down the front steps and barely have a chance to rest before she's at the bottom, a smile on her face. "You meant you'd see me here?" She asks as she pulls her ear buds from her ears and slows to a stop in front of me.

"I've been thinking about it and you're right. I need to do more if I want my movement back." She's already smiling. Her outfit today is going to be torture, but at least it made that trip down the stairs totally worth it. She has on a very tight tank top, the one with a built in sports bra that squishes her tits together and pushes them up to the top rim in the most enticing cleavage I've seen in a long time. Her tight yoga pants cling to her shapely legs and I have the urge to reach out and squeeze her thighs and pull them around me. Fuck. Maybe this wasn't the best idea. I look out at the street to distract myself.

"Great. Let's get started. We can jog really slowly. We don't need to extend our legs or put too much pressure on that new knee. Let's just keep our movements tight and focused. No need to pound." She looks me over and her attention along with all this talk about tightness and pounding I'm pretty sure my dick is about to show her just want kind of pounding he'd like to participate in.

She points up the street and then we're off. It's so much slower than I've ever run before, but it's the first time I've ran since the trauma and it feels good, like progress. She hasn't put her music back in her ears so the only sound between the two of us is our breathing. At first it was awkward, but after a few minutes I'm so in tuned to her inhales and soft breathy exhales I can practically feel them in my groin. It's slow torture. The pain is achy-- an annoying throb that reminds me I'm not a full man. I couldn't run after anyone that tried to grab her. I couldn't even win a fight right now if she needed me too. It's a very drastic change from who I used to be. I'm twenty-two years old and I move like an eighty-year old man. It's embarrassing.

"You're doing good," she encourages from beside me and I fight the urge to roll my eyes. "Knee replacement is rough—and that's without the trauma to your thigh. I think the key will be to just keep it moving a little every day."

"My right hip is hurting," I complain.

"It's from the limp. That joint isn't used to the jerky motion."

"I disagree. It's been a while, but that hip has had some practice with jerky motions." I tease, saying the words in my best over the top Ron Burgundy voice. It earns me a delicate laugh and that makes me smile. I look at her quickly because I know it's a mistake. Her skin is shimmering with sweat and each movement causes her tits to bounce and her ass to sway. Fuck it has been way too fucking long. There used to be a girl I'd train with at our last duty station. She wasn't nearly as attractive as Ashlyn, but fucking her was some of the best sex I'd had in my life. We would run until our lungs burned and our blood pounded through our bodies, then we'd tear each other's clothes off and go at it in the shower until our legs just couldn't hold us any longer.

Thinking about all of that makes me angry. I lost my ability to move fluidly when I walk and I for sure lost my ability to hold a girl up in the shower, her legs wrapped around me as I steady our bodies and pound into her until we both lose our minds. The best I can hope for is that I'll someday find a girl that loves to be on top. That's the only way I can even imagine not feeling like a total fucking failure in bed.

We round the last corner and start making our way back up the last block to my place. I don't tell her that the pain is making me want to throw up or that just doing this for a little bit is going to keep me in bed for the rest of the day. When I think I'm just about to call it quits and tell her I have to stop, we slow at my front steps. "Thanks for pushing me to go." She smiles at my words and nods her head.

"I enjoyed it. Take me up to your place." She's winded and I'm mesmerized by the rise and fall of her chest. Wait...did she just tell me to take her upstairs? My face must express my questions because she laughs softly. "I'll help you ice your knee and thigh Casanova."

"I can do it," I counter, but she's already making her way up the stairs.

"You don't have to fight everything, you know. A simple thank you would be enough." She waits for me at the top and I start making my way up. My leg does feel a little looser after the run and it shaves at least two minutes from my usual time. It feels like a victory. I show her to my front door and open it, letting her into my dark cave of depression and doubts.

"I'll grab the ice." She heads for the kitchen and I hear her digging through the freezer. "Where are the baggies?" she asks as I take a seat on my couch.

"Bottom right drawer." I almost regret not following her in there to watch her move around in that outfit. When she emerges a few minutes later with two bags of ice, I can't help but wish we were going to be using it for an entirely different purpose. I grab a pillow from the back of the couch, grateful that the lady who sold it to me when I moved in left a few of the small throw pillows I never thought I need. Watching Ashlyn's sleek, tan skin shimmering with sweat in total contrast to the way her nipples are now erect and pushing at the thin fabric of her workout top has me groaning with the sudden force at which the blood in my body rapidly converges in my dick. I'm hard in two seconds flat. Hence the throw pillow across my lap—circa seventh grade.

Ashlyn drops to her knees and I clamp my eyes shut, pressing the pillow down further and willing my dick to calm down so I don't pass out from the loss of blood to my brain. I get it buddy, it's been a long time. Her cold hand slides up the long leg of my shorts, uncovering the scars of my knee surgery. The sensation seems to climb right up my leg and under the pillow. I feel my balls pull tight in response and hope she's too focused on her task to pay any attention to the problem I'm having. When one bag is firmly in place, She slides the shorts leg up higher, but I stop her with my hand by firmly holding her wrist.

"Put it on over the fabric." My eyes are locked with hers, our breaths in sync as we begin to fall back into a pre-workout pattern. I don't want her to see the mangled mess that is my upper thigh. It's bad enough she's seen me struggle to do the simplest gym tasks, I don't want her to see what's left after being at the wrong end of a gun.

She nods her head reluctantly, but sets the bag of ice near the inside of my thigh. The cold should help my throbbing dick problem, but the view I have of her from above and how closely it resembles a girl on her knees for an entirely different purpose doesn't really allow for any humility. The cold sensation rises up and licks at the nerve endings so sensitive and ready to be stroked. When she finishes and looks up at me with her big eyes and that perfect bottom lip trapped between her teeth, I almost come just from the sight.

Part 7

Ashlyn

Would it be weird if I grabbed one of these ice packs and shoved it down my shirt? Because I'm about to overheat and that's going to be embarrassing. I made the mistake of kneeling before him and now that I'm looking up to his face from this position, my mind has begun to wander with all the filthy images that make my core feel hot and needy. I have trouble opening my eyes the whole way, the lids so heavy with the lust that hit me about ten minutes into our run.

I feel the contrast of temperature on his skin now. It's cold just outside the ice, but then burning hot where my arm brushes his skin. I want to run an ice cube all over his body. I want to listen to his intake of air and hear that groan I heard earlier coming from those lips. Beards aren't usually my thing, but that scuff on his face has me itching to run my fingers through it and give it a good tug. Would he like that? Would it turn him on to mix pleasure and pain? I feel dizzy just from thinking about it.

I release my lip from between my teeth, feeling the small indents left when I bit down as to not moan with my own desire feeling his warm breath fan out across my bare shoulders. It doesn't help that he hasn't taken those deep brown eyes off of me since I hit my knees. Damn I love a man who watches unabashedly. My nipples are pressed so tightly against my shirt it's almost painful. I hope he thinks it's from the cold of the ice and not that I want to climb on top of him and give him a little pain relief through distraction and steamy hot endorphins.

"Feel good?" I ask a little more breathy than I meant it to be.

I watch him swallow slowly, as he lifts his eyes from my breasts to my face. His own tongue moves out to wet his lips. "Yes," his low rumble is dripping with sexual tension and it pulls slightly at the invisible chord between us making my core throb a little more insistently and my body lean in closer. The tips of my breast brush his good leg and I feel the zing of pleasure race through my breasts and down my spine. I need to get out of here.

"I should go," I say but don't move. He nods his head slowly, never taking his eyes off mine. I want him to touch me. Fuck, I want to touch him, but I'm not so sure that's a great idea or one we won't regret.

"Will I see you tomorrow?"

"No. I'm off tomorrow, but we can go for another run if you're up to it. Maybe at night this time?" I don't usually run in the evening, but I'd set up almost anything to get to see him like this again.

"Sounds good. What time?" He's still looming over me as I kneel at his feet. How easy it would be to lean in again—to brush myself against him and run my hand up the cold skin between his legs where the ice is melting in the bag.

"I'll see you at seven?" He nods in agreement and I force myself to rock back on my heels and stand up. He moves to stand but I lightly push him back down onto the couch.

"I'll show myself out." I don't look back at him when I leave, but I feel the heat of his eyes on my body as I flee from his apartment and beeline for the cold relief of the shower I so desperately need.

Part 8

Mateo

I make sure to be down at the end of my steps long before Ashlyn is supposed to meet me. Watching me limp down them is not something I want her to do. I already feel like less of a man, I don't need the evidence of that to be glaringly obvious. I thought about canceling our run, but I didn't have a way to get ahold of her. She is all I could think about last night. I waivered between wanting to push her away so she couldn't see me be weak and wanting to see her again so I could have more of her in my mind to keep me motivated to get back out there.

When I see her, she's at the end of my block jogging her way towards me. Her outfit yesterday was a tease, but today it's just fucking torture. She's wearing tight pants again, but this time they only extend to the bottom of her knee letting the smooth, tan skin of her toned calf show. It shouldn't be sexy, but it fucking is. It so fucking is. I rub my face and curse at myself. I'm a grown man, not an eighth grader. Her tank top is form fitting and is currently pulling up on one side, exposing just enough of her stomach to have my hands itching to hold her there. What really gets me are her perfect tits. She has them bound down again, which only makes them fight harder to spill from her neckline. They form two perfect globes that make me want to run my tongue right along the surface.

"Ready?" She asks, seemingly oblivious to the way my eyes have been fucking her for the last five minutes. I make a mental note to not give up so easily when trying to release the tension being around her causes. Depression is a bitch. It's one of the many mental disorders that seeks to completely sabotage it's own recovery. Having an orgasm would definitely improve my mood, but feeling depressed makes getting hard a little more difficult. Add to that my disinterest in most things, and we are left with a slow start-up and an anticlimactic finish. It's been months.

"Yes. My knee's been acting up a little today, but I'm going to give it my best." She's crouched down and pulling up my pant leg before I can even finish the sentence. A wave of excitement runs up my spine as my brain recognizes this position from years of stored images of blow job after blow job. I was not a saint before my injury and I think my mind is having a hard time reconciling why we aren't partaking in one of my favorite past times.

"I can tape it for you." She stares up at me, her big eyes pleading for me to let her help.

"It's fine. I just didn't want you to be shocked if I end up on my ass during this run." I shake my leg the best I can, allowing my pants to fall back down over the skin she's exposed.

"You're terrible at accepting help." She sighs and rests her hands on her hips. Fuck. Do they have to be perfect too?

"Depends on what kind of help I'm offered," I start jogging and she quickly catches up. I feel my lips twitch at her silence. She'll learn to be careful around me.

"How's that going for you, by the way?" I'm not expecting that response. My head whips around so I can see if she's joking.

"How is what going for me?" Maybe my body has been deprived of sex for too long and now it's imagining that everything is about it.

"Sex is good for your recovery. It's good for the depression and it helps break up the monotony of trying to come back from an injury." She spouts off the information without even looking in my direction. She's not shy about it and she doesn't sound judgmental in any way. It's simply information and she delivers it like a doctor would, straight and to the point.

"Are we besties now or something?" I tease, trying to divert the attention off the topic I don't really think she'll want to discuss with me. It would go a little like: I love sex. I use it for all kinds of things. Haven't found a position yet that I don't like. Everything was just fucking phenomenal until it suddenly wasn't. Nothing. Not a touch, not a lick, not even a completed fantasy since I took the bullets to my leg.

"Grow up." She says with the perfect tone of a teen girl flipping her hair and rolling her eyes. "Tough subject?" She throws back at me and I can't decide if I like cute-innocent-helpful-Ashlyn or cut-throat-doesn't-take-any-of-my-shit-Ashlyn better.

"Want the truth?" I ask and then answer without waiting for her response. "The meds fuck me up. I'd love to get my dick wet, but right now treating the pain has to be a priority." I shake my head, "I never thought I'd ever say that." I look into her eyes this time, "The pain is that fucking bad."

Ashlyn nods her head. We reach the end of the block and turn the corner before she says anything in response. "You'll get it back. I think guys take for granted that getting off will always be easy. There's a lot of shit up here," she points to her head, "and it can get in the way of your happy ending." Our pace is slow, but steady and it makes me feel slightly victorious even though her words make my shoulders feel heavy.

"I'm just not that guy anymore, I guess." I mean that in so many ways. I never had any trouble performing no matter what was happening in my life. I was healthy, in shape, and a high achiever. I was proud of myself. The old me would run circles around this new me while wearing a weighted vest and pushing a tractor tire. As if to prove my point, my foot catches on a lift in the sidewalk and in one second flat I'm sprawled out on the pavement.

Ashlyn doesn't ask if I'm OK or make a big show of helping me up. She stands above me as I get into a push up position and press off the ground and back onto my feet. I'm almost afraid to look in her eyes because I don't want to see pity. Fuck—right now I don't think I could even handle any empathy. When I finally chance a look, her face is expressionless. She gives me a tight nod and then begins to jog again. I stand for a brief moment wondering what the fuck just happened, but then with a slight smile I take off after her. She doesn't pity me or think any less of me for the stumbles I make. She just wants me to pick my ass back up and get back to it. And for that, she just won my respect.

Part 9

Ashlyn

My heart is broken. Not tiny little crack broken, but oh my God it hurts broken. Watching Mateo fall cut me. I know how hard it is for a grown man to feel defeated even when he can hide it, but Mateo's defeat slapped down loudly and remained down longer thanks to his injury. My gut had me reaching for him, but thankfully I pulled back before he could see. I've been doing this work long enough to know that dwelling on it only makes it worse.

I covertly look at his legs while he finishes the run beside me. The fall didn't rip his pants, but there is a dark splotch of blood on his sock that keeps growing and I imagine it's from his skinned knees. I bet it's hard to go from active Marine to disabled, but he seems to be trying to figure out how to pull himself out of this injury and back into his normal life. I think sometimes that's where my patients set unrealistic expectations for themselves. He's never going to be the old Mateo, but this new one—he's all right too.

"I'm going to clean your scrapes," I say, taking his front steps two at a time while he lags behind. I do it so I'm not insulting him. If I stay back or not move to my full ability, he'll think I'm placating him. I want him to try and keep up with me.

"I'm fine."

I roll my eyes, "Of course you are." I huff a little, "You're also bleeding. You want to waste twenty minutes limping around to get the supplies and try to tend to it yourself?" I turn around and start to go back down the stairs. His hand reaches out and grips my arm. It's the first time he's intentionally touched me and I feel like my chest might explode. It's a beautiful, burning feeling right around my heart and although I can't see it, I'm guessing it would look like glitter in a windstorm—twinkling and brilliant.

"Fine. Come help." He lets go of my arm and continues his walk up the steps. I pass him and wait at the top.

"Why did you choose this building?" I ask as I for him to catch up.

"I needed to be close to the hospital. I'm not clear to drive yet." He steps past me to unlock his door and I feel the strange need to reach out and touch him again. I tangle my own fingers together to keep from making a move.

"You didn't need a place with this many stairs." I might be poking the bear at this point, but I just can't understand why he'd set himself up to be tortured every time he wants to leave his house.

His dark brown eyes stare back at me and I can tell the truth is right on the tip of his tongue. I'm practically on my toes, leaning closer to hear it. I hope he trusts me enough to share. "I'm fucking lucky to get the opportunity to go up and down these stairs. If pain in my leg is the worst thing that ever happens to me then I'm also a pretty fucking lucky guy in general." He says the words like he's thought about it a million times. I don't doubt for a minute he has. It must be lonely day after day for him, and I glance back down at the stairs that I'm sure look like an insurmountable climb every time his toes line up at the base of the first step. The wound in my heart rips open wider and now sorrow begins to seep from it, rushing into my lungs and gathering in my throat. I swallow it down.

Mateo swings the door open and gestures for me to enter. "I get to climb those stairs to get coffee or grab a beer. I get to walk down them to meet a friend and then rise with them on my way in for the night. At the top is my apartment perched above US soil. My buddy...he wasn't that lucky." His expression is unchanging.

"I'm sorry."

"So am I."

I step inside his apartment feeling like my heart weighs a million pounds. He tosses his keys from his pocket onto a small table. Then he points towards the hall to where I'm guessing his bathroom is. "All the medical stuff is under the sink. Red box." He waits for me to head towards the hall before he moves again. I find the box and pull it out, sorting through all the bandages. There are tons, evidence that his wounds used to require a great deal of dressing.

I'm holding a few items when I quietly immerge from the hall. He doesn't see me. His eyes are clamped closed and his mouth is pulled tight in a grimace. His hand rubs at his thigh. We are the same age, but when I look at him I see a life sped up by pain and loss. I know old soul refers to someone who is naturally easy going and wise, but it seems to fit here too. He's experienced so many things that take a lifetime to see—only he had it all in quick succession. It's so many losses all at once. His freedom, his friend, his mobility, his knee, and those are only the obvious things. Each like a rock tossed into a still pond, the force of the stone rippling effect after effect through his life.

I look down at the supplies and crinkle the packaging so that he's not surprised by my sudden appearance. When I lift my eyes his face is once again blank. The hand that had been kneading his injury is now fisted at his side. "This should take care of it," I announce cheerfully as I move in front of him. I roll up the legs of his pants to find his knees practically shredded. His right one is beginning to swell. He's not looking at the damage, he's look at me.

I clean them up carefully, applying a gauze pad and tape over the antibiotic cream. When I'm finished, he looks down at my work and chuckles. My brows pinch in question. "What?"

"I look like a child. I'm not bleeding to death, Ashlyn. Do we really need such a big bandage?" His smile is brilliant. It's the first full one I've seen since I've met him and it makes my own smile emerge. He's still laughing softly.

"You can never be too careful," I defend, but I laugh when my words only make his chuckle louder.

"No, I guess you can't." He folds his arms across his chest still looking in amusement at his two very bandaged knees.

"I'm a physical therapist, not a doctor." I toss a roll of gauze at him and he catches it in his fist without even looking. He definitely has the reflexes of a military man.

"Thank you for the run," he says sweetly with a genuine smile on his face.

"You're welcome," I answer proudly.

"And for the new knee pads," he tries not to laugh, but loses control. He's almost doubled over from the deep chuckles at my expense. I press my lips into a tight line and prepare to argue, but he's right. It looks ridiculous.

"Fuck off," I insist, and toss the roll of medical tape at him. He doesn't even try to catch it, only laughs harder at how ineffective my revenge was.

When he finally stops laughing, he looks up at me, "See you tomorrow?" And I can see the vulnerability in his expression. I make him sweat it out a minute before I answer. Turning to go I say over my shoulder, "Yes I'll see you tomorrow." Before I make it all the way to the door I shout back at him, "And you better be wearing the new knee pads I made you."

Part 11

Mateo

I peel the medical tape from my skin, allowing the bandage to fall away. My knee still looks swollen even though I've rested it for the rest of the day. The wound is still oozing a little, but it was only a small price to pay for getting to be with Ashlyn again. I toss the mess into the small trashcan in the corner and quickly pull the other bandage off my other knee, tossing it as well.

It was good to hear from Lucas today, a fellow Marine and good friend of mine. I've been avoiding his call and I knew if I didn't answer it after Ashlyn left, he'd come all the way here to make sure I'm still breathing. It took a few minutes for the conversation to feel relaxed, but we didn't give up. I convinced him I was recovering well and that there was no need to bring his new bride out here or even worse, leave her behind to spend any of his leave here with me. Just because I'm miserable, doesn't mean he should be too.

I run my hand beneath the water to check the temperature and then pull off the rest of my clothing. The fall this evening was a setback, but I'm determined to push through it and keep on track.

Motivation is hard when you're alone and looking at a goal that seems impossible no matter how hard you try. Somehow, meeting Ashlyn has revived the dying drive to put effort into walking normal again.

I step into the hot stream of water, letting the heat relax my tired muscles. I used to have to run long distances and through crazy terrain in order to get my muscles to protest. Now that I've been injured, it barely takes anything to make every part of me ache as if I haven't walked in years. Even my shoulders are tense. I move my head so the water runs along my neck and cascades down my back.

Closing my eyes, I picture Ashlyn. Her tight body encased in all that clingy material. It doesn't take much to remember what she looked like and the way she'd smelled like apples and sunscreen. I can see her running towards me, her dark hair pulled off her face and her cheeks pink from the exercise. I feel my dick waking up, growing interested in the images of her. Getting hard is something I used to take for granted, but now with the pain medication and the antidepressants the doctors insisted I take, it's a rare event. Well, that is unless I'm with her or thinking about her.

I keep my eyes closed, bringing up the image of her kneeling at my feet. The hot water has made my tired body comfortable again and I practically sigh with the relief as I take myself in the palm of my hand and stroke. It's been too long. I can see her lips perfectly, the way her tongue had slipped out and wet her lower lip as she worked on my knee. The blood pounds in my ears, as I grow even more rigid with the erotic image. I imagine sliding along those perfect lips, dipping inside to the heat behind them.

"Fuck," I curse harshly, increasing the speed as I fight to feel the pleasure I know I'm needed. Would she take me deep? Would she grip me with her hand to guide my length inside her mouth? My hips push forward and I feel the familiar tightening of my orgasm building. Finally. I tip my head back, letting the hot water hit my chest and pour down my skin.

My world begins to blur around the edges, my skin breaking out in tiny bumps of excited pleasure and all I can think about is getting there. My movement is unpracticed, desperate as I work towards the release that's been frustratingly allusive for months. I can picture her perfect tits and they way they would be more than a handful. My hand tightens around my dick as I imagine filling my palms with them as she lowers herself onto me. Now I'm so close I can't think straight and the steam of the shower mixed with the building pleasure makes my head light. I'm almost there.

I brace myself with my free hand against the tile, but keep my eyes closed so it's her I see instead. It's so close. I know how her hands feel on my skin and the way the air sounds as it escapes her lips when she's working hard. Up and down, up and down. My movement is getting rough, my skin sensitive and tingling with every pull. It's finally going to happen. I'm finally going to get to feel lost in the waves of an orgasm and in the satisfaction that will surely follow.

I shift my weight from my good leg to my injured one in the daze of primal need and realize immediately it's a terrible mistake. The pain shoots sharp and hot from my swollen knee like a burning dagger into my thigh. It takes my breath away. Both hands move out now, bracing my body against the dizziness and nausea brought on at lightning speed. "FUCK!" I hope on my good leg, "Fuck, fuck, fuck." I knew I aggravated the injury with the fall, but maybe it's worse than I thought. All I can think about is making the pain stop.

I'm out of the shower and dripping puddles of water across the floor as I limp to my dresser and grab my pain meds. Fuck what the label says, fuck what the pharmacist recommends, and fuck whatever restraint I've had in not swallowing handfuls of these pills before. I grab three and throw them in my mouth, biting one so it's released into my blood more quickly. I hold myself up against the dresser and wait, praying the pain will subside.

When it finally stops raging at me, I can see the purple bruising beneath the torn skin of my knee. I run my hand through my still dripping wet hair and limp over to my bed. I won't make it back into the bathroom and I can't stand up long enough to dry off. Looks like I'm going to bed tired, wet, in pain, and still unsatisfied. Fuck my life. I don't bother to turn on TV or even find my phone. I lay in the darkness wondering how much longer I can live like this.

Part 12

Ashlyn

I watch Mateo being taped up before therapy. He looks tired, the dark black circles under his eyes giving away that he didn't get much sleep. He hasn't smiled since he walked through the doors this morning and it's making me tense. I want to know how he's doing, but he isn't my patient. Instead, I help my new client get his prosthetic foot on securely, making sure it's comfortable before we practice walking again.

I try to focus, but during moments of rest, my eyes seek out Mateo. He's slower today than usual and I can see that even with the tape, his knee is still giving him trouble. When my shift is almost over, I can still see him gritting his teeth as he pushes against the weights beneath his feet. "Everything ok?" I ask Jane, lifting my chin to motion towards Mateo.

"He fell yesterday and it is pretty swollen. He stopped in with the doctor before coming in. Doc says it's just swollen, but if it's not feeling better by the end of the week he'll want to run a few tests." Jane grabs an icepack and turns to take it over to him, but her phone rings. "Can you take this to him?" She doesn't wait for me to answer her before handing it to me, accepting the call and walking away.

Mateo is still on the machine. I know he's done with his set, but he hasn't moved to the table where he can be iced. The closer I get to him, the easier it is to see the sweat that has beaded up on his forehead. He's in a world of hurt. His knee is bigger than it was when I left him yesterday, and I cringe again when I see the damage the fall did to his skin. "Hey," I say softly at his side.

He opens his eyes and looks up at me. I hold out the ice. "Hey," he answers.

"Want to move over to the table and I'll ice you?"

Mateo's eyes move down to his knee and he seems to consider whether or not he'd even make it. I watch his jaw tick with the tension of the situation. Finally he breathes out slowly and shakes his head. "Can you ice it here and then give me a minute? I don't think I can stand on it just yet." My heart dives down into my stomach with his defeated tone.

"Sure." I fetch a bandage so I can keep the ice in place and then head back over. His eyes are closed, but I know he isn't relaxing. His fists are clenched around the small handles of the weight machine and his knuckles are almost white with how hard he's hanging on. I put the cold pack on his knee and secure it with the soft bandage.

"Thank you." He huffs, flinching a little when I make one tighter round with the cloth bandage.

"I'm off in about twenty minutes if you want to wait around." I shrug one shoulder like it doesn't really matter to me if he accepts what I'm about to offer him. His eyes open and look into mine. "I can walk you home." He doesn't speak, just nods his head and then closes his eyes again.

My early morning shifts are my favorite. I love to get off work when there is still a lot of daylight left. Mateo limps slowly beside me, grunting every once in a while when the pain gets to be too much. We are barely moving as we make our way up to his place. Busy people rush past us, running to grab lunch or get back to their offices. I wonder if he notices how quickly life keeps moving even when you feel stuck. A lot of patients feel frozen in their life until the recovery progresses. It's hard to see things moving forward when everyday is a painful reminder that you aren't as quick or as independent as you used to be.

"Do you like pepperoni on your pizza?" He asks as we pass a small pizza place.

"Of course." I smile, taking another small step as he keeps up with me.

"Good. Me too. I'll order us one when we get back to my place. It will be like a celebration for not fucking limping into traffic to end this nagging pain." He's teasing, but I can tell the idea isn't as absurd to him as it is to me. He looks out into the street as a large bus passes and his lips curl up.

"You're very dramatic," I say, shaking my head.

"I'm a realist."

"I might agree if you didn't just make plans for us to have lunch. You know flinging yourself in front of a bus is only going to multiply your problems." I look up the street; suddenly seeing how far away his place is when going this slow.

"Fucking miles," he says quietly beside me, accurately guessing what I was thinking.

"One day it will seem like nothing."

"I hope so." His voice is serious. His next step is a little larger, the time he his weight solely on his bad leg will also be increased. I watch him wince, but pull through. I try to hold back my smile, but fail. I'm proud of him. I know he's hurting, but he's not giving up. There's something about his determination that makes my heart flutter. It might also be the strength I see in the body I know he believes is weak. It's not. It's injured. There's a big difference. An injured body can heal. If someone is weak, they either don't try or can't. There is nothing about Mateo that would make anyone believe he's weak.

"It's not polite to stare," he scolds.

"Then try not to look so cute." The words slip out before I even have a chance to think about them. His eyebrows lift and I can see his smile through the thick of his facial scruff that is quickly approaching a beard.

"Cute, huh?" He asks, "Do you have Nightingale Syndrome or are you just into pain?" His movement is getting quicker and apparently so is his wit.

"You're not my patient," I correct. "If it was Nightingale syndrome you'd have to be my patient when I fall in love with you."

I expect some teasing about what I said, and he doesn't disappoint me. "So it's pain then," he says deadpanned. I laugh and lightly hit his chest.

"No!" I say through a chuckle.

"Says the girl that just hit me." This time there's no missing his smile.

Part 13

Mateo

I lift my foot up onto the small ottoman in front of my couch. The pain is so much better now, but I'm not sure if that's because I doubled up on my pain meds or because I washed them down with a six-pack of beer. Pizza for lunch turned into pizza and movie and now it's beer and Chinese take-out. The sun went down hours ago and Ashlyn is still here. She's made herself at home and for some reason that makes me happier than I've been since I got here.

"So what now?" she asks from beside me. Her long legs are tucked up underneath her as she sits, turned towards me. Her eyes are a bit glossy from the three beers she's had, but she's way to cerebral right now to be drunk.

"You mean now that I'm not in the Marines?" The movie shut off two hours ago and we've been entertaining each other with all kinds of funny stories and glimpses of our childhood. Ashlyn grew up in New York, and moved here to go to school. She fell in love with the area and decided to stay around for a while. I'm grateful. She nods her head.

"I'm not sure," I answer honestly. "I always wanted to be an author. I just never had the patience to sit down and write a story. I have a few short stories completed, but if I really wanted to give it a shot, I'd like to have a full length novel to shop around to agents."

"That's great! What do you write?" She props her head up with an elbow on the back of the couch. I chuckle at her excitement. I tip my beer up and swallow it down.

"Don't laugh," I warn with a stern voice. "Science fiction. I'm obsessed with space travel." She laughs of course.

"I can't picture you writing something like that," she shakes her head and I love the way a few soft strands slip from her rubber band and fall around her face. Her cheeks are slightly pink from the beer and her eyes look even more stunning now that's she's relaxed and comfortable with me. She's not guarded. "You're too serious."

"I haven't always been." The truth is I used to be a very goofy guy. I loved space and math and reading. I used to love to crack jokes and play around just to get a laugh. "Getting injured sort of stole my sunshine."

"What stops you from getting started on a story? You have plenty of time right now to make something happen." She tucks a few strands behind her ear and I want to reach out and do it again. I want to touch her so badly.

"I don't know. It's hard to plan for the future when that requires you to look honestly at what your life will be like. What if I'm stuck here like this for a long time? It's fucking depressing."

Her brows pull together with concern, "You aren't going to be stuck here. You are getting better and I'm sure the doctor will eventually clear you to drive again." She smiles, but it looks sad for some reason. It's like a lie. "Then you can go where ever you want." I don't know her well, but I'm almost certain that idea makes her unhappy.

"Where should I go?" I ask trying to lighten the conversation back up again. I don't want her sad, it causes this tiny feeling of panic to erupt in my heart. I want to see her smile—to feel the way it soothes my heart instead.

"Where do you want to go to live the rest of your life?" Her eyes dip down to my lips for a second before returning to my eyes.

"I haven't thought about it."

"Not at all?" Her face lights up. I can see she has big dreams inside that beautiful mind.

"No, sunshine," the name slips right off my tongue and fits so perfectly she practically glows. "Where are you headed when you're done here?"

"I'm going to live in California. I want be close to the ocean and not have to deal with snow ever again." It's sounds perfect actually, and I almost laugh at the realization that I never thought about where I'd want to live because the answer was always going to be chosen for me. When I was a Marine, I would live where they told me to live. But now I had choices.

"California?" I say the name and let it sit for a minute.

"Yes," she whispers loudly. "Near the beach." I laugh and lean forward, switching my empty beer bottle for the full one Ashlyn brought the last time she went to get her own new beer. I twist off the top and toss is on the ottoman.

I move my arm to get more comfortable, stretching it out across the back of the couch and turning my chest towards her. "When do you think you'll go?" I take a long sip from my beer hoping her answer isn't in the next few months. I'd be really disappointed if I lost her.

"I'm contracted for a year. I have at least six months left before I can go anywhere. I figure I'll consider it when the time comes. If I'm ready, I'll go. If not, I'll extend my contract." She adjusts her position and it brings her arm flush against mine. I feel the connection immediately. My heart seems to pick up its pace and I can't help but twist my hand so that I can touch her shoulder. We're so close now. I have to remind myself to keep my eyes on hers and not let them wonder down to her lips too long or get caught exploring her skin.

I know it's strange, but I want to touch her hair. I want to twirl a strand around my finger and before I know it, that's exactly what I'm doing. She just keeps talking like me touching her hair is totally normal. "I have a friend that moved to California. She asked me to go with her, but at the time I was in a relationship so I didn't have the courage to pack everything up and leave." Relationship? Shit.

"At the time?" I ask. She nods her head.

"We broke up a month later. It was stupid to let the opportunity go by, but I think everything happens for a reason." I watch her dark hair twist around my finger and then spring free.

"What's the reason?" I just want to hear her talk. I'll ask her a million questions if it keeps her here this close to me.

"I don't know yet." She takes a big breath and then tips the last of her beer into her mouth and I feel my tongue run along my own lips. I want to taste her. I can taste the beer on my mine and I know it would be much sweeter on hers. She leans to the side and sets the empty bottle next to one of mine. When she moves back, she's even closer to me, our faces only a few inches apart. I feel like I'm a teenager again, desperate to kiss her and see what it feels like.

When the hair she'd tucked behind her ear springs free in her movement, I reach for it. My fingers smooth it behind her ear and I watch as her skin flushes with my touch. Her breath catches and her eyes fall to my mouth. It's all the confirmation I need that she wants this kiss as badly as I do. I watch her for a minute, neither of us saying anything, just looking into each other's eyes knowing it's only a matter of time before one of us breaks and closes the distance between our mouths.

"Mateo," she whispers almost as if it's a question, but it's more of a statement. It's a command to do what I've been holding back.

I move my lips towards hers and answer softly in the space between us, "Sunshine," and then my lips are on hers.

Part 14

Ashlyn

I know he's calling me sunshine, but I can't help but think it's also just an announcement of what it feels like to be kissed by him. It's warm and alluring, and then it grows hotter and hotter. His beard isn't unruly yet, but it scratches my skin each time our mouths move. I know woman complain about that, but I love every second of it. My hands reach up and touch his jaw, holding on to him so he won't break away. It only makes him move closer.

My lips part as his tongue dips inside my mouth and heat rises up my body in response. His strong hand moves to my cheek, holding me gently as he softly sucks on my bottom lip before pressing his lips even tighter to mine. What started out slow like a simmer, heats up to a full boil when his hand on face slides further into my hair so he can control my movement and dive further inside. I want to climb on his lap. I want to feel his strong chest against mine and know what it's like to feel the strength of his thighs beneath my own. Injured or not, I know he's every bit as powerful as I dream he is.

My heart is fluttering in my chest, my blood pumping heat and excitement through my body. He tastes like beer and perfection, a flavor that I'll now compare all others to. Somehow I know already there will never be anything better. He's a hero, a survivor—a man that knows how to use his body even when it's been injured.

I move my hands from his jaw down to his chest and rest them against his beating heart. It's powerful as it pounds against my palms, it's rhythm pulling me closer and making me crazy with lust. His hand in my hair slides lower, encircling my neck and heating my skin above my pulse. I know he can feel how quickly it beats under his thumb and I love the way he softy rubs it, as if acknowledging without words that he feels it too.

His mouth moves away from mine and his eyes stare at me, dilated and wide with surprise like he can't believe this is happening. Our chests are heaving as we suck in air. "God," he says, his voice deep and hoarse with desire, "you taste so good." His words vibrate low in my stomach and I pull my bottom lip between my teeth to keep from moaning aloud.

He moves quickly, capturing the skin just below ear on my neck between his lips and sucking. I can feel his tongue tasting me, running hot and wet across my flesh. The bite of his teeth as he perfectly mixes pleasure with pain and has me so hot with need I'm practically melting. My muscles are relaxed and my body presses into his as he guides me closer with a hand on my back. When my breasts rub roughly against his hard chest, I shudder with the sensation. I tip my head back so he can kiss and tease every inch of it.

There's this beautiful moment when I surrender. I don't care about consequences or how it might be awkward to see him at work. I can't find space in my lusty mind to even worry about how this will work out. All I know is I want him and from the way his hands are tugging at me, he clearly wants me just as badly. He moves to push me backward so he can lie on top of me, but I know the position might hurt his knee so I move my leg across his lap instead.

"Your knee," I whisper as I move to straddle him. His expression is dazed and filled with heat. His hands move to my ass and help to guide me into place. He scoots down a little further, making it possible to line my core up with his groin as I move above him. I'm gentle as I lower myself and I watch his eyes to make sure I'm not hurting him. I'm an inch above his lap when he grips my hips and pulls me down, sliding me from the base of his dick to the tip on top of his pants. Then he guides me back slowly, only to pull me forward again. The hardness between my legs rubs on all the right places and my face is instantly hot, flushed with pleasure and need.

"Is your thigh ok?" I ask softly.

He chuckles low, "Are you really thinking about my thigh right now?" He lifts his face to kiss me and tugs on my bottom lip as he pulls away. No. I'm not thinking about his thigh at all. I shake my head. "Good girl," he teases and then presses his hips forward to give me the contact I need. My back arches on its own and his hands move up to my breasts, which are now on display right in front of him.

"Mateo," I gasp his name, not really sure if it's a question or just the ramblings of a woman on fire.

"Yes, sunshine," he answers perfectly.

"More," the word escapes on a breathy sigh. His hands pull my shirt up to the top of my breasts and then tug at the cups of my bra until I'm exposed.

"You're perfect," he tells me as his eyes look into mine. He rolls the tips through his finger and thumb and I press my core against him, desperate for friction. I worry I might hurt him when I feel the hardness beneath the fabric of his pants, but he moans, closing his eyes and tipping his head back to absorb the sensation. Watching him only makes me hotter.

"I love making you feel good," I lean forward and whisper in his ear as he kneads my breasts in his strong palms.

"Feels. So. Good," he bites out as I slide my hips back and then drag them forward. He lifts his head and watches me as he licks along the top of my breasts before circling the tip, covering it in hot, wet, heat. I rock against him, so close I know one direct touch will have me falling over the edge. His hands let go of my breasts and cup my ass instead, pulling me up to my knees above him. "I want to watch you lose control," his low voice nearly making it happen. Then his hands unbutton my pants and slide the zipper down so he can pull them down my hips until they can't get any lower. His eyes take in the sight before him and then return to my gaze as his hand lightly runs along the lace between my legs.

Part 15

Mateo

My hand caresses her hot flesh through the lace of her panties. I'm hard and desperate to feel some relief. With the soft sounds she's making and the way her body is responding to me, I can't imagine it's going to take much more. Even if it doesn't work for me, watching her fall apart is going to be so fucking sexy, I know it will be the first thing I see when I finally get mine.

I begin to slip her panties down slowly, moving one side and then the other as she grips my hair and sucks in tiny breaths from the contact of lace against her swollen flesh. Finally when she's bare to me, I lightly run my fingers between her legs, pushing against her slightly to slip between her heated skin. We both moan at the contact and my hips push up reflexively, wanting to follow my fingers into the heaven they've found.

"So good," she breathes and I use my free hand to pull her towards me so I can run my tongue along her skin. I capture one tip in my mouth and suck, knowing the pain will mix with pleasure and make her dizzy. She shudders above me, pressing her hips forward and seeking the pressure she needs. My fingers find her most sensitive bundle and I begin to work small circles as I lightly capture her nipple between my teeth. When I increase the pressure she nearly loses her mind, and since I'm familiar with that desperate need to find release, I help her out. With one more powerful suck, I dip my fingers inside her, pulling them forward and cupping her as she comes apart on my hand. It might be the most amazing thing I've ever seen.

She relaxes against me her body spent and her lungs desperate to bring in oxygen. Feeling her weight only seems to drive my own need wild and I slip my fingers from her so I can touch myself. Her hand covers mine and her lips kiss my shoulder. I feel her teeth bite slightly into my skin as she slides her hips back and makes room to pull the soft elastic waistband of my gym pants away from me. The evidence of my desire is released and she takes me into her soft hand, twisting along my erection from the tip to the base.

When her tight hand rises again, lighting every nerve up with pleasure I worry that maybe I won't be able to finish. What will she think of me then? She completely obliterates that thought when she whispers, "I want to watch you now. Let me see you." Her words seem to tingle across my skin and twist down my spine, tightening the feeling of pent up orgasm in my groin.

"Oh, fuck," I groan, my eyes closing and my head tipping back as she sucks and nibbles on the sensitive skin until I feel my balls tighten. This is as close as I've been in months. Her hand slips up and down again, circling the tip and then tightening as she slides down. "Almost."

Her warm breath is in my ear and her tongue darts out to lick along the sensitive skin there. "Give it to me," she commands and then covers my mouth with hers. Her tongue dives deep and I suck on it hard as my orgasm rips through my nerves and I come longer than ever before as she works her hand around me.

Part 16

A shlyn

It was incredible to watch Mateo. There isn't a thing about him that doesn't make me want more. He finally lifts his head, having let it fall back at the end of the sexiest encounter of my life. I'm not sure how not really having sex could be the best sex of my life, but apparently he's a man that defies the rules. I'll happily be his naughty protégé. His eyes are still glazed over and his breaths are ragged and I can't get enough looking at him.

"Holy shit," he says, lifting his brows slightly as his chest rises and falls. "What the fuck just happened?"

I giggle softly at his words and answer, "I'm not too sure, but I'd like to do it again." He's already nodding his head in agreement and chuckling.

"Sign me up." His eyes are looking straight into mine and I wonder if it's OK to kiss him again. He seems to be watching me with the same curiosity. His hands are on my hips and he moves them so they are locked behind me, changing his possessive grip to a comforting embrace. "Thank you," his voice is low and sweet. "I really needed that. More than you could know."

I nod my head and then stand up from his lap. He pulls his shirt off and uses it to clean up as I put myself back together. I can't keep my eyes off him as his muscles flex and move. He's something else. I head for the bathroom to clean up myself and it's on the way there that I feel the first fluttering of panic hit. I like him. Not just the it's fun to screw around with you type of like, more like I think you're incredibly brave and wonderful kind. What if I just messed up my chance at making this something more? He seemed pretty casual about the whole experience.

It only takes the five minutes I'm in the bathroom to make the decision to keep moving forward with the friend with benefits type of scenario. He's not here permanently and neither am I. We both have stuff going on in our lives, why not help each other relieve a little stress? Maybe the more we get to know each other, the easier it will get. The rules just need to be established so I know what lines to stay between.

When I step out into the hall, he's standing with his arms folded across that perfect bare chest. He looks up at me sheepishly with a grin that melts my heart. "I'm not sure what I'm supposed to do next," he admits. I love the innocence of his statement. "I don't usually hook up with girls I'm going to see again." I'm nodding my head along with his words—it's not something I do either. "I am going to see you again, right?" he asks almost like he can't believe I meant what I said earlier. I laugh and walk towards him.

"Yes," I admit, lifting up on my tiptoes and kissing his cheek sweetly. "You're going to see me again." I rock back on the soles of my feet and smile at his bewildered expression.

"OK," he confirms, reaching out and touching my hip so he can pull me closer. "But am I going to get to touch you again? Are you going to touch me?" My chest feels so full of excitement and giddiness. Our bodies are now pressed closely together and his hot stare is focused on my eyes.

"Most definitely," I answer. His lips rise into a bright smile that I can see through the scruff of his beard. "I need to get going, it's late." I say the words but can't quite convince my legs to move when my skin is tingling at every point of contact I have with him.

"Goodnight, sunshine. I'll see you tomorrow." He presses a soft kiss to my forehead and releases his hold on my body. Well, at least the physical one, because when I step back from him it still feels like he has me. It's like somehow I gave him something of mine, and he handed over something of his that will keep us tethered together. I'm not sure what to make of it yet, but I already can't wait for the next time our lips meet.

"Goodnight." I turn and let myself out of his apartment. I don't stop moving until I get to the end of his block. I'm afraid if I look back he might be there and I won't be able to resist coming back for more. It will be too soon—too much. At the same time, I know if I look back and he's not there—it might just break my heart a little.

Part 17

Mateo

I slept soundly for the first night in a long time. I had stood at my door and watched Ashlyn leave until I couldn't see her anymore. The protector in me hated that I couldn't walk her home, but she was in a hurry and it would have taken her at least three times as long to make the walk with me by her side. It's because if that, today I woke up early and increased my exercise routine. I'm going to get this leg back to normal so I can walk her home.

I open the door to physical therapy and immediately find myself scanning the room for her. I find her leaned over Levi again and I want to walk over and kiss her stupid right in front of him. It's going to be fucking torture to watch her help him when I know that guy only enjoys PT for the show she doesn't know she puts on. As I stretch, I can hear her laugh. It's interesting that I even like the sound of it as much as I do. A lot of girls I've been around try too hard and their laugh is forced, not light and flirty like hers.

I'm pushing myself hard, not that I wasn't before last night, but now I see there's a reason outside of my own selfishness to get better.

I want to be worthy of her and to do that; I need to be the best I can. I take a short rest in between sets and she brings Levi over to help get him set up on a machine next to mine. She gives me a small wave and I smile back. I'm not her client, but I don't know if she's allowed to have any romantic relationships outside these doors with clients of this place.

"OK," she tells Levi, "Three sets of twenty this time."

"Sure thing," he answers. His eyes stay trained on her as she sets up the machine. I can't watch it so I turn my head away and press up to begin my set. "I'll be right back, Levi. I'm going to get another patient set up. You've got this, right?" He nods his head and starts his set. We both work in the quiet for a few minutes. The only sound is the clanking of metal as the weights tap each other.

"She makes coming here worth it," he finally says, turning his head in her direction. CLANK. My weights slam together as I release the resistance a bit too quickly. "She seems real young to be a therapist." I've known Levi for a while. We've been training here for months now and I've never had any problem with him before. I try to remind myself he doesn't know about us. No one does. Fuck, I don't even know about us. What the hell are we doing?

"You think she has a boyfriend?" he asks. Levi is older than I am probably by a few years. He's too old for her. Even if he's not, it's just not happening.

"Probably. She's too pretty not to," I answer as casually as possible.

"Maybe she's keeping her options open," he waggles his brows and I want to punch in in his mouth. "I'll ask her."

I rest my hands on my knees and stare at the wall. If I get up and walk away right now it will be awkward, but I'm not so sure I want to hear her answer or hear what Levi is going to ask in return. She's not mine, I get that, but I don't want her to be anyone else's either.

"How's it going?" she asks him when she returns.

"Good. A little sore but getting better." I chance a glance in her direction and catch her looking at me. She turns her eyes to Levi again when he asks, "Do you have a boyfriend? I know you don't have a husband. No ring." He's pretty proud of himself for that one. I shake my head and start my next set.

"No. I'm single. I don't really have a lot of time to date." She watches him to make sure he's using the right form. I feel the heat of anger in my chest for no good reason. What did I think she was going to do? Tell him we messed around and were planning on doing it again?

"Dating isn't a chore when you're doing it right," Levi informs her. "Maybe just grab a drink or something sometime." He's working his way up to asking her out and now my pulse is hammering away. I feel my teeth grit together and my jaw tighten as I lift the weights and try to ignore their conversation.

"I go out," she laughs. "I just don't have anyone I'm serious about right now." Now you can add panic to the mix. Anyone she's serious about? Does that mean there are other men? I didn't really ask that before we practically mauled each other last night. Dammit. She rests her hand lightly on his knee, adjusting his position slightly and then moves to get his attention off her. "What about you? You have a girl you're seeing?"

"Nope. I'm a free man myself." His answer makes me roll my eyes even though I know it's childish. I let the weights clink together again and then sit up, carefully stepping off the machine in an effort to get away from their conversation before I get really pissed. She's done nothing wrong. I didn't ask her to be exclusive and she didn't ask me to be either. We never even talked about dating so really the only thing I can do is hope she wants to have more fun together and take what I can get.

I set the weights up on the next machine and sit down. My head is spinning and to be honest, I feel a bit nauseas over the whole thing. If I wanted to have a talk with her about it, it should have happened before we hooked up. Now anything I say might freak her out. It might make her think I'm coming on too strong, too fast. I close my eyes and breathe out slowly. I need to call Lucas later, or maybe Liam. The two of them have been great at helping me get my head out of my ass and back into getting better. They also both happen to know a thing or two about women.

My knee is feeling better, but not where I want it to be. I've kept it iced and was meticulous with the stretches the doctor showed me and now all I can do is wait for time to heal it. I scratch at my beard and run a hand through my shaggy hair. I barely even recognize myself anymore. I turn my attention back to the machine and slide a pin out so I can adjust it to my height. I smell her before I see her at my side.

It's the crisp smell of apples again and I find my lips curling up before I even move my eyes in her direction.

"How's your knee doing today?" she asks softly. I lean back on the bench and turn my head so I can see her. She's perched n the machine next to mine, her bright smile perfectly in place. I want to kiss it. I want to so bad I feel myself leaning closer, but it can't happen here. Her eyes dart up in my therapist's direction. Jane is good at what she does, but they have too many people assigned to her caseload. She teaches us and then sets us up to work independently. It works for me, but sometimes I worry about the younger guys with worse injuries. It's fucking hard to pick yourself back up—literally. She should be around more for them.

"It's been better."

"Let me show you something," she says, leaning over me and fuck if my whole body doesn't zip back to life. I have to grip the plastic beneath me so I don't grab her. It would be so easy to touch her face and pull her lips to mine, but then we'd be in big trouble. Instead I just let her adjust my ankle and run her hand up my calf. She watches me and I feel so fucking crazy because I can't tell if she's really trying to help me or if she just wants to touch me and I'm really fucking hoping it's the latter.

"You're leg should be lined up like this," she says the words as she moves her hand up my leg and I'm powerless to do anything but watch. Her hand tucks into my pocket quickly and then she stands back. "I think you've got it now." What the fuck?

"Seriously?" I ask. She just shrugs and gives me that smile that makes me stupid. I can't think of words or movements...nothing but smiling back. I watch her leave, her perfect ass encased in the stretch fabric. I have no idea what that just was. I press my legs for the beginning of the set and feel a new sensation in my thigh. I slip my hand into my pocket and feel a piece of paper. That sneaky girl. I want to read it immediately but I can't without it looking totally random and having everyone watching me unfold it. So I'm left to finish my session full of anticipation.

Ashlyn doesn't say another thing to me for the rest of the time I'm there. We catch each other's eyes a few more times, but not even so much as a smile is exchanged. I hate it and love it all at once. Something about the sneaking makes it so much more exciting, but then I remember that no one will know she's off limits if no one knows she's mine. Then I remember she's not really mine either.

By the time my session is over I practically burst through the doors so I can read the note. I pull it out of my pocket on the front steps and unfold it like it holds all the answers to every test I'll ever have to take.

Saw you walking this morning on my way in. You made me proud.....and hot. Like I want to hug you for the effort and then kiss and touch you until we can't breathe. Call me later. You know if you want your hug....or whatever.

She included her number and a smiley face. It makes me laugh. Maybe I should take the high road and tell her making her proud does this funny thing to my heart. It makes it grow and swell with pride of my own. I should tell her I that I'm a good guy and I'd really like the hug she offered.

Instead my excitement and relief get the best of me and I text her:

Hey sunshine. I'd like to cash in on that "whatever."

Part 18

Ashlyn

It shouldn't be sexy to watch a man on a leg machine, his brow gleaming with sweat and his muscles bulging from the effort. It shouldn't be so hot to watch him move his mouth as he breathes or bite his lip against the pain. It shouldn't, but it really, really is.

After Mateo leaves I get his text message, Hey sunshine. I'd like to cash in on that "whatever." My heart quickened its pace and my face grew warm with the thrill. At the end of my shift, there is a huge possibility that I will get to have his hands all over me again. It's all I can think about for the rest of the day. I'm obsessed in the best kind of way.

I give up trying to get any paperwork done and slide my finger across the screen of my phone. I bring up his text message and reread it for the tenth time. I look at the clock and see that I'm almost free. The anticipation has me excited and eager to get out of here so I can go see him. I decide I may as well pass the time doing something fun because nothing on any insurance claim form is going to get me distracted from the image of Mateo I have playing over and over in my head. His mouth slightly open, his eyes glazed and staring into mine expressing such a raw need and appreciation for me.

Me: I was just thinking about you...

Mateo: That sounds promising.

Me: Did you know that your eyes get even darker when I'm touching you?

Mateo: That's because all the thoughts behind them are dirty. Did you know when I'm touching you this little breathy sound escapes your lips and drives me insane?

Me: Maybe it's my body's way of trying to cool off. It gets pretty hot when your skin is on mine. Did you know that my new favorite flavor is the taste of your skin below your beard right before your neck meets your shoulder?

Mateo: Are you sure? Maybe you should taste a few more areas before you decide that. I should probably find my favorite flavor on you. I have a good idea of where I want to start.

Wow. Like OMG wow. I fan my face quickly, scanning the room to make sure no one is watching. I'm a forward girl, but I've never done anything like this before. Usually sexting isn't my thing, but with Mateo it only helps heat up every image of him that plays through my head. When the clock finally strikes leaving time, I'm packed up and out the door before anyone can stop me. I head in the direction of his place, pulling out my phone with the intention of asking him to meet for dinner.

Mateo: You've been quiet for a while. It's not my favorite sound. I prefer my name on your lips as you lose control. Come over and let me see if I can make you say it again..and again.

Me: I'm on my way. I'll say your name after I make you say mine.

Mateo: You first sunshine. Ladies are always first.

I knock on his door, turned on and hoping we can skip any formalities and just get to the dirty part. We can figure out everything else later. My brain can't focus on higher level thinking, it just wants his hands on me, and my mouth licking every part of him. The door swings open and Mateo tosses his phone on the small table next to his keys. He reaches for my hips and pulls me through the open door, pushing it closed behind me. Without a word he slips my purse from my arm and takes my phone and places it next to his. When there is nothing left to occupy our hands, we fill them with each other.

Mateo pushes me against the door, his mouth on mine at a desperate pace that has me heating up and melting in his touch. His fingers dig into my hips like he can't get enough and I tangle mine into his hair and pull him closer. My lips are swollen already, our tongues dancing and licking—drawing us in until there's barely room to breathe. "I. Want. You. So. Fucking. Bad." He practically growls in the moments our mouths part for air. And he didn't have to say anything because I can already feel it between my legs and in the heat of his hands on my body.

"Hurry." Is all I can say, tipping my head to the side when his tongue licks a hot trail down my neck. The scratch of his beard makes my skin pebble with excitement and my head grows dizzy with anticipation, lust and so much fucking need I think I might explode right this minute. My hips tip up on their own and one of my hands leaves his tousled hair to grip his ass and pull him to me.

"Mmm." He moans, taking a second to slowly thrust his own hips forward rubbing inch by inch his erection against my core and I'm sure I'm going to incinerate. I feel the blood rushing to each sensitive inch of skin, heating and swelling, bringing to life a delicious ache that I know only he could satisfy. It makes my hands greedy, my palms fisting into his clothing, yanking and pulling him until I can't think straight.

"Shirt," I manage, tugging past his roaming hands and over his head. As if he just remembered he could do the same, he removes mine and tosses it to the side.

"Off," he commands, unclasping my bra and pulling it down my arms. His fingertips along my skin ignite the nerves and douse the burning ache in gasoline. This time when our mouths meet, I have the fleeting thought that I could do this forever with him. Then his hands dip into my waistband and annihilate and chance at thinking anything else besides now—I need him now.

Part 19

M ateo

Her skin is heated beneath my palm, a light flush stretching out up her neck and across her cheeks. I can see the red marks where my beard has scratched her and I'm feeling a strange mix of guilt and pride—sorry I hurt her but so happy I've left my mark. I pull her waistband away from her skin and let my fingers brush all along the top of her panties before I pull them away too. She's soft and a beautiful combination of feminine and strong. I've never been with anyone like her and I know she's going to ruin a piece of me for any girl after.

I push the fabric down her legs as far as I can with my limited flexibility. She never falters, picking up where I left off. She kicks her shoes off then tosses her pants and panties to the side, somewhere near where I threw her shirt and now she is standing brilliantly naked in front of me.

I close my eyes and try to hold back a smile, "You know," I whisper, "if you weren't so pretty I could make this last a little longer." I laugh, completely comfortable with her already. She laughs too as she slips her hands beneath my shorts and boxers, pushing them down as she grabs my ass.

"And if you weren't so cute, I'd make you take me out a few times first." She's full on giggling now and I love it. I like making her laugh and I like that she has the same effect on me.

"Thank God for that then," I say through a smile. My lips are back on hers in such aggressive pursuit she has to rest her head against the door so I don't knock her over. She drives me insane. I feel crazy for her. My feet are already bare so finishing the task of removing my clothing is easy and quick. Her hand moves down my side, over my hip and starts to slide lower.

I'm not a narcissistic guy, but my pride just can't get past how awful my thigh looks. When her fingers tease the skin beneath my hip and dance their way down to my upper thigh I completely tense up. My hand is over hers in no time at all and I stop her from letting them move any lower. I pull back from the kiss and watch her face. She seems hurt and I hate that. My heart feels attacked in my chest.

"What's wrong?" she asks tenderly with an edge of concern. I'm not sure how to tell her. I haven't really even spoken about it with anyone. I know it shouldn't matter, but it does. I pull her hand up and hold it between mine.

"It's bad,"

Her brows furrow in question and she stares into my eyes as if she'll find the answer there. "What's bad?" When I don't answer her it only takes as moment for her to realize what it is that I'm not saying. "It doesn't matter to me." She pulls on her hand, but I don't release it.

"It does to me." I can't believe in the heat of everything I forgot about keeping it covered. I feel exposed and vulnerable. Both are feelings I despise.

"I'll close my eyes," she offers sweetly. I shake my head. She's quick to finish the thought I didn't know I was interrupting. "Just long enough for you to get your boxers. I'll close them until you're covered." She doesn't wait for my answer—doesn't give me a chance to say no. She just shuts her beautiful, forgiving eyes and stands still. Her naked body before me is just as vulnerable as mine, but she trusts me. I don't move to grab them right away because I can't take my eyes off of her. It's not even just what she looks like, it's the way she holds no judgment. It only confirms what I've known all along. Ashlyn isn't just gorgeous on the outside; she's remarkable on the inside too.

"Thanks sunshine," I whisper and I know she thinks I'm talking about letting me cover my scars, but really it's so much more than that. I grab them from the floor and slide them back up my legs. It's not graceful at all. I know there has to be a few times when my foot thuds loudly against the floor as I wobble on my unsteady leg when she wants to open her eyes and reach out to me—but she keeps her word. And then something strange happens. I think that I'll feel less vulnerable with my cotton boxers as a wall between the ugly part of me and her beauty, but what she just did has stripped all the armor I was wearing and I stand before her more vulnerable than before.

Part 20

Ashlyn

There is a lot of ugliness in this world, but a scar received while fighting for your country could never be one of them. Mateo's physical therapy is going well, but his mindset isn't healing as quickly. It breaks my heart, but I won't let him push me away or use it as an excuse to keep his distance. The scratch of his beard is on my cheek right before he kisses me. I open my eyes and find his staring back at me.

His hand reaches out and cups my cheek, his thumb rubbing tenderly in a circle. His lips are back on mine, determined and with renewed purpose. He shifts his weight completely off his bad leg and I realize standing the way we are after a long day of working on building his strength might be painful. "Couch?" I ask between kisses.

His hands find their way to my hips; his lips never leaving mine. He tugs me forward as he backs up to the couch behind him. My hands are in his hair and his hands are sliding up my body, touching every inch. He drags his fingers across my breasts, over my shoulders and down my back. I let mine wander too. I feel the smooth skin over his pecs and down his stomach. I don't let the boxers get in my way, pulling them down again just enough to release him.

"Sit down," I say and direct him with my hands flat on his chest until he begins to lean back. He has to let me go so he can use his upper body strength to sit down and stretch his injured leg. He smiles up at me and opens his arms inviting me to join him. I move closer, but I don't sit. I lean forward and kiss his lips, loving how quickly his hand is tangled in my hair, pulling me closer and lifting his face to mine like he can't get close enough.

His hand is hot where it touches the inside of my knee. My heart rate soars again. This man has the power to light my fire with one little touch. He lightly grazes my skin with his touch, inching up at a pace so slow I'm desperate to feel him at my core. I rest my hands on his knees because I worry my own will give out the second his fingers find my sensitive area. I'm not wrong. His fingers slip along my center, the first pass being so light that I can barely feel him and yet it's enough to wake up the nerves and send them into a crazy flurry of tingling sensations that race to climb up my spine.

His fingertips slip between the swollen flesh, coaxing the bundle of nerves into responding with a shudder and throbbing pulse. My eyes close against the pleasure and I drag in a strained breath. He traces the tip of his nose along my cheek, his beard scratching at my flushed skin until I turn into him, too desperate for his mouth to wait for his to come find mine.

Mateo parts his lips and my tongue dips inside, meeting his and pressing in further to show him just how crazy with lust he makes me. His response is perfect, his tongue taking the lead and pushing into mine showing me with each touch what he wants to do to my body. His fingers slip inside. First it's just one slowly sliding in until I can feel his palm against me, but he never stops. He pulls back, dragging along every nerve inside until he can slide another finger in again. I have to remind myself not to dig my nails into his skin at his knees.

It's a slow torture that I never want to stop. He's playing me so perfectly I might never survive it. My heart is pounding, my pulse thumping in my veins, rushing my blood to the parts of my body that are now aching with the need to find a release. Only now that I've felt his hands on me I know that the need isn't just for any release, I want a release brought on by his touch.

His free hand grabs my ass and then moves down, rubbing the backside of my thigh before guiding my movement to part my legs wider. When he has me positioned how he wants, he holds the side of my face and sucks on my lower lip until it's released with a satisfying pop. "Hold on, sunshine," he warns, his fingers in my hair tightening until I can feel the pull at my scalp. It's not much of a warning and I don't have time to react, but I don't care—I'm thankful even. He's going to finish what he started and it can't happen soon enough.

His lips touch mine with dominance, guiding my mouth open and then joining our tongues. It's hot and exciting, mindless pleasure that makes my knees grow even weaker. His fingers between my legs quicken their movement, sliding in and out along the bundle of nerves until I can't think of anything but letting go. Even though the pleasure takes over and the euphoria drugs my system, he doesn't relent. He leads my mouth through the choppy movements as I reach my peak and then finally when it hits I moan into him, my own release heighten when his low groan answers sending wave after wave of bliss through by body.

*****Vote! Your votes and comments on this chapter will determine how hot Mateo's chapter gets.

Part 21

Mateo

She sighs into my mouth, her body relaxing under my touch. My body is doing anything but relaxing. Now that my focus isn't on the way she feels or the little sounds she makes, I can feel my own ache. I'm surprised I can think of anything in the shape I'm in. I doubt any blood flow has been reserved for thinking—instead it's throbbing in my groin insisting on attention.

I move my hand from between her legs, leaving the one in her hair at the back of her head. Give me a break; I'm not really operating on a fully functioning brain. Her heavy lidded eyes look into mine and they are only made ten times more beautiful by the bright blush on her cheeks. Her lips are parted as she inhales and exhales with purpose. When her tongue darts out to wet her lip I audibly moan. Nothing has ever turned me on more—no dirty pictures, no raunchy pornos—nothing.

I thought it was the hottest thing ever...until she begins to kneel. I have to close my eyes to even stay in the game. If I watched I'd be a goner. Her warm palm takes me, wrapping around and squeezing with just the right amount of pressure to make me jerk beneath her fingers. I let out a big whooshing breath, tipping my head back and looking up to the ceiling, praying this moment never ends.

There is so much need and pressure building beneath her grip I worry that my whole body will combust when it finally tips over the edge. I feel the soft tickle of her hair brushing along my bare knee and I have to bite down hard on my lower lip to counter the most intense pleasure ever with pain as she licks the tip with a delicate swirl of her tongue. DAMN. My chest expands and my hips lift, seeking to be buried in her warmth.

When the wet heat slides over my entire length, my head rights itself and I stare down at her with all the wonder of a teenage boy getting his first blowjob. I can't think, hell, I can't breathe now. Her tongue slides flat and moves up, down and all around in this wonderful technique that has me teetering at the edge of my release in only a few seconds. I tell myself she'll understand if I let go now. She'd have to after what I just watched when my fingers were between her legs. Right? Please? My eyes shut again, but I lose the battle and let them open, albeit small since they are so heavy with lust I have to fight to keep them open at all.

Her hand returns, first with just a light brush against by balls then more insistently as it wraps around my shaft and slides up in a chase behind her plump lips and unbelievable tongue. I might pass out. I might actually die of a fucking heart attack before this whole thing is over. And believe me when I tell you—it was so worth it. Every little palpitation of my heart, every indent of my teeth into my lip and finally, every bit of fluid lost when I'm finished will all be worth it.

"Sun..." I try, but the air is pushed quickly from my lungs when her tongue licks over the tip again. "Sunshine almost..." It's no use. I can't speak. I just surrender to her.

The last clear thing I take in before the hammering of my own pulse is all I can hear is a sexy little moan letting me know she's ready. And then with all the force of every muscle and cell in my body I hold on and let go all at once.

Part 22

Ashlyn

We are doing this whole thing backwards and it leaves me wondering where we go from here. Normally it's dinner, then kissing, then hooking up. For us we started at the hooking up and now find myself in the bathroom, staring at my reflection in the mirror. I see my red cheeks and silly smile, but I can't seem to find any regret for what I've just done. I'm sure it will hit me someday, maybe when this is all over and I'm left with nothing but memories of steamy hook-ups.

Mateo knocks on the door and I shut of the sink. "Yes?" I ask, my heart racing with anxiety about what he might say. Is he going to tell me to go home? Will I be able to hide the disappointment on my face?

"Do you want a burrito or enchiladas?" His voice carries through the door and maybe that's why I don't believe I heard that correctly.

"What?" I turn the knob and open the door so I we aren't speaking through it.

"Tostadas get soggy before they get here. The taquitos are pork—not beef," something I can tell he doesn't agree with by the disgusted look n his face. It makes me laugh. "Tacos are good, but not as good as the burritos or enchiladas. So which will it be?" For the first time since we started this conversation his lip twitches and then curls into a smile. He's nervous too and it's so cute.

"Are you inviting me to stay for dinner?" I ask, folding my arms over my chest.

"Well I certainly don't want your stomach growling through the whole movie."

"A movie too?" I wasn't about to admit how happy this made me.

"It's not going to watch itself." He said the words like they weren't crazy and my heart did a little flip in my chest.

"What are you going to eat?"

"Burrito." He holds up a small delivery menu and points to the third item. I can't contain my own smile as I shrug my shoulders.

"Then I'll get enchiladas so we can have half of each." I'm looking into his eyes, loving the little wrinkles around the edges as his smile grows.

"I knew you were perfect, but I had no idea you were also brilliant." He pulls his phone from his pocket and dials the number. I follow him out of the bathroom and into the living room. Our clothes are back on, but I can still see his strong biceps as he leans his upper body against the small bar that separates the kitchen from the living room. He lifts his chin, directing me to sit on the couch. I turn around as he orders our dinner, but I don't find a seat right away. Instead I head over to the small table in the corner by a window.

I didn't really look around the last time I was in his apartment and now that I'm in here again, I want to learn more about him. He has a laptop out and open, but the screen is dark. Next to it he has a notebook, worn and torn at the edges. I want to open it so badly, but I don't. This is his space and I'm just a guest. There are a few post-it notes stuck to the top of the table with handwritten messages that make no sense at all to me, but I imagine are part of his story.

I run my finger across three dates written on one of the notes and then my eyes catch on another post-it tucked partly beneath his laptop. It's my name all in caps. I can see where he's traced over the letters multiple times. The gesture makes my heart swell and happiness bubble up beneath my cheeks until I'm smiling so big they heart.

His voice from behind startles me, "I'm not a stalker, I promise." I turn around and see him standing with one hand in his pocket and the other on the back of his neck sheepishly. "It's been helping me through my writers block." He peeks at me with his chin tucked into his chest like he's waiting to be scolded. He couldn't be more wrong about how my name from his fingers makes me feel.

"You've been writing?"

Mateo nods his head and slips his hand into his other pocket, rocking back on his heals and reminding me of a young boy answering to his teacher.

"That's great. What are you writing about?" I take a few steps towards him until he's looking down into my eyes.

"You'd think I was crazy if I told you." His eyes move from mine down to my lips, stopping there for a moment before rising to meet my gaze again.

"Try me."

"It's about a recluse cop who stays shut inside, nursing a bum leg while solving local murders." His hand moves towards my face slowly and I close my eyes when the back of his knuckles brush lightly across my cheek. His touch warms all through my body and my stomach flutters like it used to when the boy I was crushing on would talk to me.

I open my eyes. "What's so crazy about that?" I reach up and hold onto his wrist, keeping his hand touching my skin.

"Because no matter how fucked up his life is and how limited he lets his world get, he still falls head over heels in love with his partner." I love the idea already, but can't quite see why that would make him crazy. He watches the question play out in my features and chuckles softly when my brows pull together in confusion. He runs his thumb gently across my bottom lip, following the trail with his eyes. I part my lips and he reads the signal perfectly, leaning in and kissing me slowly. It's different than any other kisses before and I have to remind myself to keep my feet planted on the ground because I feel like I might float away. When he finally pulls back he grins shyly, "I named her after you."

Part 23

M ateo

"So do you have an agent yet?" She asks as she holds a spoonful of ice cream in front of her mouth. It takes me a minute to process her words because right now all I can think about is how badly I want to be that spoon. She slips it into the mouth I am now familiar with and I watch her perfect lips as she closes them around the cold metal. I thought this wild attraction would wean off, but it doesn't. I want her again and I already know even the next time won't be nearly enough.

"No. I have to finish the novel first." I follow her tongue as she licks the drop of chocolate from her lip.

"How much have you written?" She looks at my ice cream and then moves her spoon to my bowl and retrieves a bite of the mint chip I have instead of her chocolate. "Mmm," she moans and can't help but laugh out loud. "What?" she asks seriously.

"You have no idea do you?" I point my spoon at her and she shakes her head. "You're like a walking wet dream. All bouncing boobs and sexy moans. You can't even eat ice cream without being sexy." I steal a scoop of her chocolate, holding out my bowl to her so she can have more of my mint.

"Yeah right," she rolls her eyes. "My hair is all messy and this outfit is something a tired mom would wear." She tugs at her tight shirt and looks down in disgust at her yoga pants. "I look like I didn't give any shits today about who might see me."

"You're beautiful. You could be wearing a trash bag and I'd still want to have sex with you." I reach over and wipe a small drop of mint ice cream from the corner of her mouth.

"Are you trying to tell me you're into trash bags? Is that some fetish you get off to?" she teases.

"I'm into whatever you're in. Trash bag, yoga pants, lacey panties. ..." I shrug my shoulder, "Come to think of it, I'm also into nothing. Like you could get naked again and I'd be totally into that." It earns me a light punch to the arm.

"Tell me more about writing. Are you getting close to being ready for an agent?" I'd worry she was just trying to keep the conversation going so it doesn't get awkward, but she's looking at me with a very serious expression and I can see that she genuinely cares about what I have to say. I think about it for a minute.

"I'm about half way through the story. I was stuck for a while, but that changed." I smile and quickly take another bite of ice cream so I don't give away just how happy it makes me to be back at it—and that she is currently my muse.

"That's so cool!" she practically screeches. "How often to do you write?"

"I started the story when I couldn't sleep. I think I created a character with a disability because I was trying to make sense of my own. Sometimes when I get insomnia I write a few chapters. I don't really touch it much during the day." I set my bowl aside.

"Do you know how you are going to end the story?" She scoops the last bite from her bowl and holds it out to me. I take it and then I grab her bowl and wait for her to put her spoon inside. I swallow and lick my lips as I set her bowl to the side with mine. She is patiently waiting for my answer.

"I have no idea." I can see that she's cold, tiny bumps covering her arms and neck. I grab the blanket off the back of the couch and wrap it around her. "I've never written anything as long as this story. It started in a pretty dark place and I'm just trying to stay true to the characters." I rub my hands up and down her arms on top of the blanket. I can smell the faint scent of apples; the fragrance is something that makes me feel this weird mix of arousal and contentment.

"I'm impressed." She says the words quietly and honestly. I stop my movement and look at her. Her words make me feel proud. Pride is a feeling I used to be very familiar with. I was great at sports my whole life and felt pride for the goals I accomplished playing. Then I felt proud to be a Marine. I guess I never realized how much I missed that feeling until feeling now.

She looks so cute wrapped up in my blanket, her pretty face framed by her dark hair. "I'm in trouble," I reply quietly. I can't fight it any longer and I let my fingers swipe across her forehead, down behind her ear, and along her jaw. She doesn't say anything and I worry for a minute that she might try to bail. We haven't discussed what's happening between us and my words might be all the information she needs to figure out that I'm not so confidently standing on the friends with benefits side of the street as I was the first time we hooked up.

It's not my fault. I've never met anyone like her. She's smart and nurturing, fun and so hot it burns my heart. I tried to keep it casual, but looking at her now I know my words are true. I'm in trouble. I want to touch her all the time. I want to feel her under my fingers and hear all the little sounds she makes. I want to memorize the way her face looks when she's looking at me and I want to know what it's like to fall asleep with her in my arms. If that doesn't show you how much trouble I'm in, I don't know what will.

There's nothing that's going to keep me from handing Ashlyn my heart on a silver platter. I have to focus for a minute to make sure I haven't done it already. It's not like me to get this hooked on a girl. I'd like to say I don't know what it is about her that has me this sprung, but I can't say that. I know what it is. It's the way she understands me already, the way she takes time to wait for me. It's the way she didn't give up on me and pushed me to want more for myself. It's the way I think about her at night and how she's the first thing on my mind in the morning. It's all the little things that have me tripping over myself to see her smile or hear her laugh. I'm so into this girl it's embarrassing.

She lets the blanket fall from around her shoulders and slowly puts her hand on my knee. It's a move that before my injury I wouldn't even consider a come on, but having her do it makes me feel better, proud that she finds me worthy. I don't think there's anything she can do to make me stop falling...but then she slides her hand up to my thigh and the floor of my perfectly comfortable room falls out from beneath my feet. All I can think about is the way my scars must feel beneath her fingertips and the world around me begins to spin. I feel nauseous and overheated all at once. My stomach twists and pushes up towards my throat and my heart stings with the jolt of panic then beats so quickly I worry I might pass out.

I stand up from the couch like it's on fire and step back, stumbling when pain shoots up my leg. I grab the deformed muscle tightly, taking a few half steps until I gain my balance back. I'm afraid to open my mouth for fear that I'll throw up everywhere so I find myself shaking my head instead. No, it's not you. No, I'm not OK. No, I can't do this.

"I'm sorry," she says, her eyes immediately glassing over with tears and I hold up my hand to stop her before her voice laced so deeply with pain and disappointment can pierce my already damaged heart. It's not her fault. I'm the crazy one. I'm the one who can't stand to be touched there and can't seem to get past this. I hate it. It makes me feel weak and unworthy. I take another step back.

I've never been great with words, but I'm absolutely terrible with them when I'm having a panic attack. I can't get my mouth to open and the words I want to say are lost in the spinning and rolling. I try to rub the pain from my thigh, but the heightened awareness the panic brings only makes the pain there more noticeable. I feel the sour burn of vomit at the back of my throat and I know the adrenaline and pain are mixing up a perfect storm of misery. I turn quickly and limp towards the bathroom, closing the door behind me before bending over the toilet. I hear the front door close in the distance, and then my world goes dark as not for the first time since my injury, I pass out.

Part 24

Ashlyn

I run all the way home. I don't stop and wait for it to be my turn to cross, only look for traffic and then time it so I can run between the cars. My face is cold in the night air and the tears on my cheeks feel hot as they slip down and fall from my jaw. It's all too much. It's too overwhelming. I'm too invested.

It shouldn't have mattered that he freaked out on me. We are just now getting to know each other so he doesn't owe me anything. I knew about his thigh, but as much as it must feel like the most important thing in his life, sitting there with him I'd already forgotten about it. It's not like his injury made him unlovable or disgusting. I tried to be understanding at first, but knowing he sees his injury as something to be embarrassed of or that I'd be repulsed if I felt it beneath my hand really hit too close to home.

I take my front steps two at a time, pulling my keys from my purse which is slung across my body. Once inside, I toss my keys on the kitchen counter and start stripping off my clothing. It's clinging to my sweating skin and making me feel claustrophobic. I rip my shirt over my head, unclasp and toss my bra in just a second and then shimmy out of my panties and pants. I turn on the shower and let the water heat up until the bathroom begins to fill with steam.

There was once I time I couldn't look at myself naked either. I remember just after the crash, the way my body had felt disgusting—something that once was mine that I no longer recognized. I'd worked hard to overcome that cognitive distortion. Now I can look in the mirror or run my hand along the bumpy scars without worrying that they make me less human or ugly. I turn away from the mirror, but look back at it over my shoulder. The long raised scar starts just below my right shoulder blade and gashes towards my spine in a jagged path.

Maybe it helps that I can't really touch it myself. I can only look at it and imagine the way it might feel to my own hand or someone else's. What I do know is how the one on the back of my calf feels to my touch. I've ran my fingers along it so many times over the last six years that I've memorized every bump and each hard knot. It's pink now, a lighter color than the previous purple it once was. It runs from just beneath the back of my knee to the inside of my ankle.

I remember the pain there after the sound of crumpling metal had stopped and I was trapped upside down, hanging from my seat by the seatbelt that had saved my life. Blood trickled from the cut and dripped off my knee, landing on the bashed in roof of the car as the sirens rang out in the distance. I hadn't felt the pain in my back from the slice of metal that had pierced my seat from behind and dug in as the car behind ours pushed the trunk all the way up to my back. I know what it's like to be scarred. I know what it's like to think you will never be the same person.

We started our relationship from the wrong direction. We should have gotten to know each other first. He should have heard about the accident and the wounds it caused so that I might have learned how ugly he thought scars were. Had I known that scars were so horrifying to him that he couldn't even deal with his own, I would have never started anything with him. I close my eyes and turn my head back around. I play through all of our encounters, shaking my head at how awful the whole thing might have gone if he's seen the scars I've worn for a long, long time. Watching him be so turned off by his own, I know that if he'd seen mine it would have been just as horrible or even worse.

I step into the shower and let the water wash over me. It's been a long time since I've felt ugly, but tonight that is exactly how I feel. The scars that have been a part of me for years now feel like marks of unworthiness and I reach for the rag hanging over the spout and lather it with soap. I run it along my skin, pressing hard to try and wash away the ugly puckering of skin at the very end of the scar on my leg. I know the tears are streaming from my eyes, but I don't stop. I scrub and scrub until I finally collapse on the shower floor, rolling into a ball and letting out all the tears I thought I'd never have to shed again.

Mateo might have been trying to protect me from his scars, but he inflected new ones on my heart, my soul, and my delicate sense of security with my own body. When the water runs cold I don't care that my roommate Rhett is working nights, because right now I want to be covered instead of making my usual naked walk to my room. It's a need to hide that I thought I'd gotten over. I wrap my towel around my body and head for my room. I chose a long pair of pajama bottoms and a thick shirt that I know will cover the thick damaged skin. I climb under my covers and close my eyes tight, praying that in the morning I'll get out of my bed after a night of forgetting all about Mateo.

Part 25

Mateo

When I open my eyes my head pounds with the force of a million bulls charging inside my skull. I struggle to get up off the ground, my bad leg is stiff and I feel immediately that I twisted my knee again. This fucking leg is never going to heal right. I pull myself up on the bathroom sink and notice the knot on my forehead and the blood that dripped from the cut just above my right eyebrow and down along the side of my face. It's still wet so I must not have been out for very long.

I rinse off my face and grab the first aid kit out from under the sink. I dab some hydrogen peroxide on the wound and then close it the best I can with the little butterfly Band-Aids. I open the medicine cabinet and pour a few Advil in my hand. I toss them back and scoop some water from the faucet to wash them down. They might help my headache, but they are going to do nothing for the pain I feel in my chest. I hurt Ashlyn and for that I will suffer all night.

I don't bother with a shower because I don't trust myself to stay on my feet long enough to finish it. I limp to my room and peel off my shirt. I'd take off my pants too if I thought I could do it without falling down and making this night even worse. I pull back my covers and climb inside them. Looking up at the ceiling in the quiet dark, I come the closest to crying as I've been since the night Pines was taken from us. I'm a fucked up mess and I let it push Ashlyn away. I have no idea how to fix it.

I reach for my phone on the nightstand and dial her number. It only rings once before going to voicemail. I laugh without humor because I know that means she saw my number and sent me straight to her messages. Damn it. I open up the message window and watch the curser blink while I try to figure out what I could say that might explain my crazy behavior. We are getting to know each other, but we are not to a place where I can spill my guts to her about why I really hate that part of my body. I'm piss at myself that her hands on me got my head spinning and my stomach lurching up my throat.

Me: Sunshine I'm so sorry.

I wait for her response, my stomach jumping with anxiety and heavy with dread. Maybe I freaked her out. Maybe she ran out of here scared of me and has no plans to ever talk to me again. I hate to admit it, but that would break me. I might not be in love with her, but I know I need her.

Me: You didn't do anything wrong. I can't look at that part of my body. Scars are ugly reminders. Just looking at it makes me sick.

I pull at the hair on the tip of my head, frustrated when she doesn't answer that text either. Do I keep explaining or just let her go?

Me: Sunshine please talk to me.

When she doesn't respond to that, I leave my phone on my nightstand and shut off the small lamp. She wouldn't understand and I don't have the words to explain it. In the darkness I admit to myself something I have been trying to avoid for months. My scars remind me of the day I watched my friend die. It's less about the ugly skin and missing muscle beneath than it is about me living while he died. The bullets fired from his killer hit him in the head, and then the rest of the magazine was emptied into my leg. It should have been all me.

I roll over and bend the pillow around the back of my head so that I can use it cover my ears. My own thoughts are so loud I can't escape them, but the outside sounds I can drown out. I listen to my pulse pounding in my head, the throb from where I must have hit the bathtub is still beating away on my forehead. I feel tired quickly, like I've been drugged and I close my eyes trying to push out the thoughts of Pines and all the blood. I remember they way ours mixed together as I cradled his head on my lap. The last place he rested was on my mangled thigh and now I'll never be able to see it as anything else besides the place where he laid to die.

Part 26

A shlyn

I wake up on Monday with the start of a cold. I know that most people would go to work with the symptoms I have, but I also know how hard it is to work on strengthening your body when you feel terrible so I stay home so I don't risk making anyone else sick. Rhett is usually asleep until around noon, but when I wonder out of my room I find him at the kitchen table, eating a bowl of cereal and scrolling through his phone.

"Good morning," he says around a bite of his breakfast.

"Morning. I hope my coughing didn't wake you up." I finally got out of bed around two this morning to take some cough medicine. He just shrugs his shoulders, too nice to admit I had.

"Did you call in sick?"

"Yes. I thought I'd just hang out here and try not to give everyone this bug." I grab a bowl and spoon and head over to the table. I'm still in my pajamas as I take a seat across from him. He stops eating and pours me some cereal and then tops it of with some milk. I take a bite and try not to meet his eyes as I chew. We've been best friends since high school and I know it won't take long for him to figure out something isn't quite right.

"Do you want company today? I was going to meet up with Georgia but I can change my plans." I can feel his eyes on me. I shake my head.

"It's OK. Go have fun." I manage a smile and finally gather the bravery to lift my face.

"I don't..."

"Rhett." Now my eyes are directly on him. I say his name like a period—shutting down his words before he can say them.

"Something is wrong. I can see it all over you. Are you going to tell me about it or do I get to worry all day about you?" He sets his spoon down and folds his hands in a steeple over the bowl. He knows I hate soggy cereal, even when it's not my own. I eye his bowl and then huff out a sigh.

"I met someone."

Rhett nods his head. He doesn't pick up his spoon yet, a sign that he isn't finished with me just yet. I laugh a little and he smiles, knowing he's making me crazy thinking about how mushy the milk is making his flakes. He lifts his brows and leans forward, a not so subtle hint to keep going.

"Fine," I laugh. "He's recovering from an injury to his thigh."

"You really are going to try and save everyone aren't you?" He shakes his head and I roll my eyes. He's always on my ass about my need to help other people who have suffered an injury.

"It started as that," I tell him honestly. "But then I started liking him." I shrug one shoulder and take a bite of my breakfast, dropping my eyes to his bowl because I can't help myself. "We have this chemistry that's undeniable. We hooked up a few times, but then he freaked out."

He slowly picks up his spoon and I imagine he's trying to decide how much of this story he wants to hear. It can be hard for both of us to listen when it comes to our sex lives. He clears his throat, "What do you mean he freaked out?" His voice is low and it puts me on edge as I register the warning in it. I shake my head immediately, rushing to finish my bite so I can correct his assumption.

"Not about that. He hasn't seen them yet. I touched his leg on accident—well, on purpose, but I forgot about his injury. He stood up like I'd burnt him." His face relaxes a little, but he's watching mine to make sure I'm telling the truth. I've had men in the past be total assholes about my scars. One guy I went home with said he couldn't go through with it once he got a good look at the scar beneath my bra.

"What's the story with his leg?"

"I don't know. We haven't talked about it yet." He chuckles and raises his spoon to his mouth. "You're such a guy." The spoon slides in over his lips and I narrow my eyes at him. We always tease each other and living in this small apartment has made our private lives nearly non-existent. I can hear everything even when his bedroom door is shut, and I cringe to think that the same goes for my room.

"I hope your flakes are soggy," I say immaturely, but it earns me a genuine smile.

"So what are you going to do?"

"I don't know yet. If he is freaking out about me seeing his scars because he hates them, then what will he see when mine are on display?"

Rhett's eyes trail down my body. He takes his time examining the whole picture. "My guess is that he is going to see a smoking hot body that someone takes very good care of. He'll see your perfect skin, perfect ass and perfect tits. If he notices the scars it will be nothing compared to what he will see that he likes." He keeps his eyes on me as he takes another bite of his cereal. He and I are not sleeping together, but sometimes we talk like we're in an intimate relationship. I think it's because I was the only girl in our group of friends and all the boys talk to me like I'm one of them. Sometimes it makes me cringe—there are just some words a girl doesn't want to hear, but most of the time I appreciate the brutal honesty.

"I don't know. It's ben so long since I even thought about what a guy might think. What happened last night has really messed with my head."

"And your choice of pajamas." He scrunches his face up like they offend him. I reach for a coaster in the middle of the table and toss it at his head. He makes me laugh and before too long, we are both cracking up.

"What's so bad about my outfit?" I ask when we are finally calming down.

"I just prefer the little boy shorts and tight tank top. You look like my mother on Christmas morning." This time my laughing turns into a coughing fit. He stands up and takes both our bowls to the sink, returning with my box of cold medicine from the cabinet. "Are you sure you don't want me to stick around?"

"Get out of here," I tell him with a smile. He hesitates for a minute and I think that maybe he's going to say something else. Instead he bends down and kisses my cheek.

"Text me if you need anything." Then he heads back to his room. I watch him go, smiling at easy it is to forget he's a transfemoral amputee. The crash that scarred my body crushed his leg. Before you feel sorry for either of us, it's important to mention that I walked away, Rhett survived but struggled to walk, and Joseph never took another breath or walked again.

Part 27

Mateo

I haven't been able to take my eyes off the door since I walked in here and saw she was nowhere to be found. My stomach is in knots wondering how I'm going to fix this mess now. I finally fell asleep last night around 3am, but she never responded to my texts or called me back. I want to ask why she's not at work, but I don't want to make Jane suspicious.

I'm just finishing my set when Levi rolls in. He is met by one of the other therapists and they have a small conversation I'm too far away to hear what is said and I want to growl in frustration. I don't want to talk to Levi about her because knowing he's thinking of her makes me irate. I hate her name on his tongue. At the same time, not knowing if she is OK is making me insane. I watch Levi set up on his first machine and I casually make my way over to the machine next to his.

"Hey, Levi. What's up?" I sit down and play with the weights.

"Nothing much. I'm cleared for surgery. I hope this one will be the last. How about you? How's your thigh man?" He looks at my leg but of course it's covered. I don't ever leave it out for people to see. I'm not ready for all the questions that will come of it.

"Good. Still really tight, but I feel like it's getting better." I set the weight and push up for my first set. Levi does the same beside me. We don't talk through our set, but when it's time to rest he turns to me.

"How's your head?" He taps his forehead and I think he must be talking about my new wound.

"Oh, that? I hit it yesterday. This leg makes me unsteady." I touch the Band-Aids and feel the bruise beneath.

Levi shakes his head, "I'm not talking about the outside." His voice is monotone and almost ominous. He keeps his eyes on mine and appears to wait for me to understand just what exactly he was talking about. I feel the sweat start to bead on my head. I've made it a long time without anyone questioning what the incident might have done to my mental health. When we were being debriefed before heading back stateside, they made us fill out a bunch of forms and check off a few things on these generic checklists. I must have passed because I was never questioned about it again.

I turn my face away from his and start another set. As my thigh burns, I consider my options. For some reason, I feel myself starting to crumble from the inside. I've tried not to talk about that day, but I'd be lying if I didn't say that it was creeping up on me. My dreams were constantly a perfect sequence of the same events that took place that day. I also find myself staring off into space, thinking about everything from the weather that afternoon to the smell of the blood and burnt flesh. I lose hours of time lost in the memories of that loss.

"You know," Levi says without looking at me as we try to catch our breaths again. "I was recommended a group for trauma survivors when I first came here. I turned it down and was pissed that someone thought I would want to it around and talk about that fucked up day or hear about other peoples' trauma. But then I could get it out of my head, you know? I just couldn't shake it. I've been going for a few weeks now and it helps. I can't say it's going to cure me, but at least I can talk about it with other Marines that know what it's like."

I'm frozen now, looking straight ahead so I don't have to meet his eyes. I know in the Marines we call everyone "brother," but I just can't see talking to a group of wounded men, How are they going to give any shits about what happened to my friend that day? They have their own stuff to work through. "I'll think about it," I tell him and he gives me a tight nod. I push off again and add a few more to this rep. Maybe if I push myself the pain that's currently a low ache in my limb will demand to be heard above everything else in my head.

When we're both done and wiping the sweat off our machines with small towels, Levi stops me before I move on. "The group meets again tomorrow in room 189." He lifts his chin in the direction of the hall outside the front doors. "8am."

"Thanks," I say without committing.

"And she's sick today. They've planned for her to stay home all week." He gives me a knowing look and then wheels himself to his next machine.

Part 28

A shlyn

Jane told me to stay home this week to make sure I don't get anyone sick. They've called in another therapist to cover my shift, but I need to stop by quick to make sure my client files are updated with the treatment plans so she can follow them. I duck into my office and handle it quickly. I haven't spoke to Mateo since the night I left his apartment. He usually isn't here this early in the morning and I want to make sure I'm out before we run into each other.

I'm almost clear when the door at the end of the hall opens and the trauma group that meets there on Tuesdays begins to spill out. There are men and women of all ages in there given that it is an open group that allows members to drop in and out as needed. I stay close to the wall so the wheelchairs can get by and I'm sure to keep my eyes low so I'm aware of crutches and prosthetics. Eventually most of the amputees who are putting work into getting stronger will walk as smoothly as Rhett does on his. The first six months after the accident he was very depressed. He hated that all of his movements were stilted and that people felt they needed to give him miles of space to get by.

To him it was insulting and embarrassing. I will always remember that and work hard to not make any one feel like I'm uneasy around them.

"Sunshine," his deep voice came from the end of the hallway and I look up to find him standing between my quick exit and me. I'm not prepared to see him, and my heart starts to flip flop while my stomach clenches and then feels weighted down in my gut. I feel drawn to him, my arms wanting to reach out and pull myself against his chest. I've missed him more than I want to admit. I'm not quite sure how that can be since we've only known each other for a short while. I wonder if maybe our history of trauma has made us kindred spirits.

I don't say anything, a lump in my throat making it too hard. Everyone is moving along, leaving the hallway empty except for the two of us. It dawns on me that he is leaving the group room. My heart squeezes in my chest and I feel a small ray of relief that he's reaching out and getting more help. I know first hand how hard it is to put yourself out there like that. I'm still in contact with a few of the people from my trauma group, and I live with the guy who invited me to my first session.

He takes a few tentative steps towards me, but my feet are planted and I can't get them to move. "Can I talk to you for a minute?" he asks sweetly. I nod my head and see the relief in his eyes. I motion for him to follow me to my office. We walk in silence and step inside. I close the door behind us and wait for him to speak. "I messed up," he admits. His eyes look tired, red and rimmed with dark circles. I almost reach out to touch his face. His beard is getting longer and it makes him look wild some how and that makes my insides warm.

He takes a step closer to me, "I don't like talking about that day." He looks away quickly and I can see the way his body tenses and his heartbeat thumps quicker where I can watch it just above his collar. His hand moves up to rub the back of his neck and I can see him struggling to say the words. "My head is full of all these details," she takes a deep breath and clears his throat. I can hear the emotion in his words and voice. "I can remember the smell—first the livestock. We were all talking shit about how the heat made the air thick with the stench of animal shit." His face twists in disgust. "I remember having a headache. It was hot and we were low on water so the sun was just pulling it from us and our uniforms were trapping in the heat."

I watch the man before me struggle with what he lived through that day and my heart aches for him. I want to make it better, but know that I can't. He looks into my eyes with a sad smile, "I, um, I heard the first shot clearly. There was so much other noise. I heard the shot but it was too late." He runs his hand up over his head and pulls at it like causing pain will center him.

"It's OK. We don't have to do this all today." I step closer so that I have to look up at him. His eyes seemed lost, so much pain behind them as he looked down at me. He nods his head and let his hand fall.

"I just need you to understand it wasn't about you," he reaches for my hand I let him take it. He flattens it between his own and brings it up to his mouth for a kiss. He's tormented by what happened and

I realize that it was less about his scars and more about the memories I'd triggered when he felt my skin against his damaged thigh.

"I get it," I say pulling my hand from his. He looks stung again, but I shake my head. I turn around and lift up the back of my shirt. I feel vulnerable, but I need to show him I understand about the scars you wear on the outside and how they are nothing compared to the ones you feel on the inside. I close my eyes when I know he is looking for the first time at my scar. I move my shoulders so my shirt will slip down again, but the warmth of his fingers on my back stops me. He traces it gently, his fingers moving over the raised skin like it was still delicate. "I have one like it on the back of my leg, too." I turn around and face him again.

"I had no idea."

"I know," I say, forgiving him. "It's been a long time. Mine are old, but yours are still new. Take all the time you need to fix the inside." I rest my palm flat against his heart. "You can't do much about the mark it leaves on your skin, but you can change how deep you let the roots on the inside grow."

"What about us?" I want to tell him that we'll be fine. I want to reassure him that we will both be able to put those experiences behind us, but there is never going to be a day that we won't carry what we lost.

"I'm still here," I smile up at him but I feel my lip quiver slightly with the knowledge of what I have to do. It's best for the both of us if he works out his issues without trying to balance me too. I learned that the hard way. "Fix this first," I say so soft it's almost a whisper as I softly rub his chest. "Right now the pieces of your heart are scattered everywhere. I won't take any of them until you're sure there's enough left for yourself." I swallowed down the tears I felt stinging my throat. I might not know everything about him, but I know what it's like to have one minute completely shatter your life and everything you thought you knew about yourself. It tears from you your innocence in thinking you're invincible and that stories about losing friends could only ever be just stories.

Mateo touches the side of my face, letting his thumb rub softly across my cheek. He watches me carefully and then nods his head once in agreement. "I'll get better and then I'm coming for you." He smiles, but it was the saddest expression I've seen on his face since we met. He leans in slowly, giving me a chance to stop him, but I can't find the strength. When I tip my chin up he finishes closing the distance and brushes his lips across mine. My lips part as his coax them open and I feel their heat dance down my spine and along every cell. He might call me sunshine, but it's just a reflection of the warmth he gives me. His kiss is tender and when he pulls away I start to miss him already.

Part 29

M ateo

Two months later....

Torture. That's exactly what I wake up for every weekday. I'm up early, working my walking speed up to a steady jog. The pain in my thigh is still there, but it's way more manageable than it was in the beginning. I'm still staying at my apartment near the hospital, but it doesn't feel like a prison cell anymore now that I have parts of my day I truly enjoy. My days are usually the same, I get up and go for a jog, attend my physical therapy, come home and shower and go meet a friend or sit my ass in the chair in front of my computer and write until the words blur together.

The only time my routine changes is on Tuesday mornings. I have attended every group since that day Ashlyn spoke with me in her office. Sometimes it's hard. Really fucking hard. Before the group I only had to struggle with my own depression and trauma. Being a member of the group has expanded that to empathizing with other wounded warriors. It's a lot, but it's working and feels very rewarding. At first I kept my distance, not really letting anyone in, but after the first month, I looked forward to going and even met up with a few of the guys around town for coffee or beer. The lonely gets a little smaller each time I get out of my comfort box and allow some human connection.

The torturous part of my day is when I open the doors to physical therapy and have to spend an hour or more in the same room with Ashlyn. She's still my brightest ray of sunshine, and not reaching out to her or tasting her lips on my own is maddening. I'm not sure how much longer I can do this without losing my mind. She and I will smile at each other and even wave now and then, but that's the extent of it. She's keeping her distance and while I like to think we could be together and I could continue to get well, she has the scars to prove she knows best. I've learned to trust the people who have already walked the path I'm taking.

I open the doors and look for her, like always. It's a habit I'm not in a hurry to give up. She's working with Levi, bent over in front of him fixing something on his wheel chair. He looks up and me and gives me an evil grin. He's been fucking with me for the last two months. He knows I have it bad for her, but can't do a damn thing about it. Levi and I have actually become friends outside this place so he has the inside story as to why I'm always so tense and frustrated when she's around me but not with me.

Jane has added a few new exercises to my routine now that I'm getting stronger. I walk to the mat, my steps so much smoother than the first day I set foot in this place. I still have a bit of a limp when I get going, but if you didn't know what to look for, I might be able to pass as normal. I lie on the mat and pull my knee up and let it fall to the other side of my body. This stretch used to hurt so bad I thought my muscle was being torn from the bone. I've gained a lot of flexibility and I'm going to work every day to not lose one centimeter of it.

The scent of apples sweeps past me and I close my eyes and picture Ashlyn. At first it was images of her kneeling before me, or her flushed cheeks as she held herself over my body. Now I picture her laughing, or the excitement I saw in her eyes when I told her about my novel. Don't get me wrong, the other images are still there—I just save them for times when I'm alone. I move my leg back and lift the other, stretching it across my body. I can feel eyes on me, but I don't want to look because if they aren't hers I'm going to be disappointed.

My phone vibrates in my pocket and I drop my knee back and read the message. It makes me smile unreasonably big. I feel the excitement pump through my body. I type out a message in response.

Me: I can't wait. Let's get drunk and start some trouble!

The response I get makes me chuckle. I finish my stretches and stand up. I see Ashlyn across the room. Her eyes meet mine and she looks sad. I feel my own smile fall. My phone vibrates again and she watches me retrieve it, but then turns back to the patient she's helping. I head for the bike. I love that I'm limber enough now to do something other than walk at a granny pace. I type out another response.

Me: You coming alone?

I'm not ready to add an incline yet, but peddling the bike is getting easier. This time the text message makes me laugh out loud.

Me: Don't worry. We can snuggle. I'll keep you warm.

I tuck the phone back in my pocket and focus for the twenty minutes I'm on the bike. I can't wait for tonight. I need to relax, get loaded, and have a really good time. And tonight, I have the perfect date. With the excitement of tonight running through my head, PT seems to go quicker than usual. By the time I'm on my last exercise the happy feeling I had just minutes ago is being replaced with frustration once again. Ashlyn won't look at me. It's not the usual keep our distance type of ignoring me; it's deliberate and cold. I don't take my eyes off of her as I start the last set. She has to turn around at some point. I watch as she demonstrates a squat to a patient. Her ass looks amazing her pants, but I don't let it distract me from my mission. She is going to look me in the eye before I leave here or I'm going to be miserable this weekend.

"What did you do now?" Levi asks as we both rest on our machines. He's staring at her too.

"Right?!" I say harshly. "Everything was fine when I came in here. Now she won't even look in my direction. It's making me crazy." I push against the machine and the weights clank loudly with my uneven movement. She looks over her shoulder at me finally, but it doesn't make me feel better. It's not the playful flirty look she usually gives. Her eyes are cold and her mouth is a straight line across her beautiful face. "Damn it," I growl and Levi chuckles.

"I don't think I've seen her like this since the first few times the two of you clashed heads in here." He lets out a low whistle. "She's even hotter when she's pissed."

"Fuck you," I tell him and he laughs.

"No thank you. I got that all handled with my date tonight. But I recommend you take care of that on your end before you break the damn machine." He slides up just as I slam back down. I'm f*cking done. This girl has me twisted and turned upside down. Levi's right about one thing, if I don't let off some steam, I'm going to explode. I don't stop walking until I'm out on the front steps. The air feels good and I stop to take a few deep breaths. My phone buzzes again and I pull it out to read the message. I hope it's Ashlyn even though we haven't text in months, but I find myself smiling even though it isn't her name on my screen.

Part 30

A shlyn

I pull the hem of my little black dress down as Rhett and I walk into the bar. It's not my usual scene, but after today he said I needed to get out of the apartment and back into life. He reaches for my hand and pulls me up to a chair, leaning in very close to yell in my ear over the loud music.

"What drink will obliterate him from your mind tonight?" He brings his face right in front of mine with a big grin. I love him for this almost as much as I hate him for making me do it.

"Vodka should do it," I answer with a smile. I tug the hem down once more and he stares at my cleavage and shakes his head.

"Quit tugging that dress down. If you tug it any lower your tits are going to fall out the top. I won't complain, but I don't think that's the look you're going for tonight." He slips his fingers into the top of my dress where my boobs meet my underarm and tugs it back up with a fatherly look. I stick my tongue out at him.

"I wanted to go out in my jeans," I remind him loudly.

"What fun would that be? You are supposed to be out here letting loose and looking for a man." As if he only reminded himself that he should be looking for a hook up too, he scans the bar.

"I don't want to look for anyone," I say it more quietly than before, hoping he doesn't really hear me.

"It's been two months, Ashlyn. Either get with him, or get with someone else. I can't take how tense you are. It's so bad that I feel the sexual frustration." He turns his attention back to the bar and the pretty bartender. "Four shots of Vodka, a Jack and Coke and a Vodka cranberry."

"What the hell, Rhett? I want to get buzzed, not slip into a coma!" He hands me my shot with a shrug of his shoulder.

"This should loosen you us a bit." We both take the shot, our faces pinching with the sting of it. I feel nothing. He hands me another shot and hold his up to toast with mine. "To getting you laid." He clinks my shot glass and we both down the Vodka. It hits all at once. My face feels heated and a warm sensation spreads out from my stomach to all of my limbs. He watches me with satisfaction.

"Better." I agree. He hands me my drink and leans in again, his chest against mine thanks to the crowd of people packed into this tiny bar.

His hand holds me firmly at the small of my back as he tells me, "You look beautiful tonight. If he saw you he'd want to do whatever it took to make you his. Let's just have some fun and solve all the world's problems tomorrow." I close my eyes and nod my head. When I open them, I can see the way the bartender is watching Rhett. She meets my eyes in apology but I shake my head with a smile and mouth, "Not mine."

Rhett spins me slightly as he tells me, "We've got a live one, missy. That guy has been watching you since we walked in here. I think if I don't let you go right now he might even try to kick my ass." He laughs and takes a step away. "Go get him tiger," he teases as he points back to the bar. "I think I might just grab a drink or two...maybe a few digits." So he had noticed the bartender. I bite my lip and nod my head. I hold my two fingers up like a peace sign and Rhett checks his watch. "See you at 2am unless I get lucky!" He shouts and I turn to find the man he was talking about. It only takes a second for our eyes to meet.

Mateo is standing near one of the tall bar tables, watching my every move. His eyes look hungry and possessive like he just caught another kid playing with his toy. I know it should make me angry, but instead I feel my cheeks flush hotter and my tongue slides across my lip. His eyes leave mine as they look me over from my lips to my toes and then back. It's hot and exciting, but when they meet mine again I see something else inside them. Jealousy? Anger? I'm not sure.

I break our eye contact and look around trying to find another familiar face in the crowd. He wasn't supposed to be here and now I want hide. I can still feel him watching me and when I look back at him, he folds the little red straw of his drink over the rim of the glass and pounds the entire thing, setting the empty cup down on the table. His three friends are now looking at me too and I have no idea what I should do about any of this. Finally one of the guys at the table elbows him in the side and says something I can't make out. Mateo shakes his head and turns around to face his friends, shutting me out completely.

Part 31

Mateo

"Don't lie to me asshole," Garver demands over the loud pounding music. He looks back at Ashlyn and shakes his head. "That's her isn't it?"

I have my back to her now so I just shrug my shoulder and the whole table erupts in laughter. "Holy shit," Smith says over his drink. That look you guys were giving each other was so hot I almost finished without touching myself." The laughing gets louder as Garver and Lee offer high fives. Yep, we are all a bunch of sixth graders. They think it's funny because they hadn't seen her when she first walked in. I watched that guy hold her hand and lean down to talk to her. She let him tuck his fingers into her dress, practically touching her boobs. I want to rip each one of his fucking fingers off and shove them down his throat. Nope, instead I'm just going to throw up.

My stomach turns with discomfort and my heart feels like it's trapped between a vice and someone is twisting the handle. I'm guessing from the murderous look on my face and the fact that I'm not laughing, Garver can see that something isn't right. He slides his drink over to me and then pries the drink out of Smith's hand as well and sets it in front of me. With a disgruntled look, Lee passes his drink down too. I slam them back one at a time.

"What did I miss?" Garver asks when I finish the last of the alcohol at our table. I crunch an ice cube aggressively between my teeth.

"The douchebag that had his hands all over her. He held her hand then he felt her up. Fuck this." I set the glass down and wait for the alcohol to dull the pain. It doesn't. If anything, it just makes the fire in my stomach burn hotter. He has to be her boyfriend. Her date at the very least. I hate him. If I weren't so in to her, I'd hate her too. It would be easier that way. I turn back around and feel my stomach roll once more when I can no longer see her. I look through all the people before seeing her at the bar.

Ashlyn is standing beside him, her face red and her arms moving quickly as she tells him something. He has his arm around her waist protectively and I want to rip it off and beat him with it. In fact, that's just what I'm going to do. I take a step, but Garver grabs me by the back of my shirt.

"What the fuck?" I shout, but he just pulls me to my chair. Smith is laughing again and I consider punching him in the face.

"That's like his signature move," he says.

Garver is looking at me seriously, "Come up with a plan before you stomp someone."

"My plan is to murder him. All better?" I try to move but he doesn't let me go.

"She wouldn't have looked at you like that if she was with him." He tries to reason with me, but the panic inside has taken off and I'm imagining all kinds of bad scenarios where she has a boyfriend and hasn't told me.

"It happens all the time. Girls lie." So do boys. No one can be trusted. I make a note of that in my foggy drunk mind.

"I'm not buying it. Go talk to her and figure it out. We'll be here if you need us. Don't get us into any fights. I need to be on that plane in three hours, not sitting in a cell next to your stupid ass."

He lets go of my shirt slowly like he's unleashing a wild animal. I straighten it out and roll my shoulders back. He's right. I just need to get o the bottom of this. I find her at the bar, but she turns and heads for the hallway where the bathrooms are. I stalk after her and I swear the guy at the bar smiles like a jackass when I pass him. If I wasn't afraid she'd disappear, I might stop and feed him his teeth for dinner. I think of everything I want to say to her. All the questions I need to ask are forming in my muddled mind as I enter the dark hallway.

She's about two steps ahead of me on her way to the girl's room. If this had been months ago, I would have never caught up with her. But now, I move quickly and efficiently—especially when I'm after something. Just before she can reach the girls room, I grab her arm and spin her around. I mean to say her name. I mean to ask her all those questions I've come up with, but when she's in my hands and staring up at me things don't go as planned.

"Sunshine," I manage to growl out, but then I can't think of anything else besides how much I want to kiss her. I can't find the words to tell her how mad I am and how fucking ruined I will be if that asshole out there is her boyfriend. I guide her back towards the wall so that we aren't blocking anyone and so that I can press her up against it. And then I cover her mouth with mine, finally doing what I've needed to do everyday for the last two months.

Part 32

A shlyn

He tastes like whiskey and every fantasy I've ever had. His strong hands hold my arms, pinning up against the wall as his mouth presses onto mine—demanding and surrendering all at once. I part my lips for him and love the scratch of his beard against my soft skin. He pulls away slightly, tugging my bottom lip between his teeth. His hands slide down my arms until he has my wrists and he lifts them to the sides of my head, releasing his hold so he can intertwine our fingers. Then he moves my hands in his above my head.

He rests his forehead on mine, his eyes still closed as he breathes me in. I know exactly what he's doing because I'm doing the same thing only I'm watching him, captivated by the need to experience his next move. He kisses my neck while he moves one leg between mine and presses in on me, truly pinning me to the wall with his body. It's sexy and possessive and I feel like I might pass out from the rush. "Mateo," I whisper, wanting my hands back so I can feel him.

His warm mouth sucks the skin at my shoulder and I squeeze his hand in mine. The alcohol in my system is making everything more intense. I can feel the roughness of his face, the strength of his chest against mine, and his firm thigh between my legs. I tighten my legs around his, tipping my hips to allow the denim of his jeans to slide up my inner thigh. If I move much more the bottom hem of my dress will be around my hips and I'll be flashing anyone who walks down this hall. The funny part is I don't care. I have him here, in my hands and I won't let anything get in the way of us right now.

His teeth nip at the soft skin of my neck and goose bumps break out all along my flesh. I turn my face into him, pulling his ear lobe into my mouth until he can't fight it any longer and he lifts his head allowing my mouth to surround him. My hands are going numb from the tight hold he has on them and their position above my head. He shifts his hips forward and I can feel where he is hard against his zipper as it rubs up my thigh towards my hip. It's delicious anticipation. I'm practically chanting to myself, more, more, higher, closer. A flush races up from my stomach, across my chest and spreads out over my cheeks. It's like a fire is burning hot and white inside me and if someone doesn't put it out I might go up in flames.

His lips are back on mine, nipping and pulling. His teeth graze my tongue and my lips and my own tongue pushes past his swollen lips to find the warmth of his mouth. We aren't thinking or planning—just crashing together in a hot mess that has been brewing since the day he walked through the doors of my work. He is everything I've ever wanted and now that he has his hands on me I never want him to let go.

"Tell me," his voice is rough and demanding. He doesn't finish before his tongue is back in my mouth again and I arch my back so that I can feel him all along my body.

"Tell you what?" I ask desperate to say anything he needs me to say. He doesn't answer. His mouth is too busy connecting to mine, melting me from my lips to my toes.

"Tell me," he demands again. And this time he pulls back, his face looking dazed and his eyes so heavy with lust only a small portion of their chocolate color shows from beneath his lashes. "Tell me," he starts again and hesitates like the answer to the rest of his command might be bitter on his tongue. "Tell me he's not your boyfriend." He kisses me again before I can answer and my heart hurts for him. I know if I were to say he was, he'd be shattered. I know because I feel the same way about him. He finally pulls away from me so he can look in my eyes. I'm speechless. All the emotion I see in them makes it hard to breathe.

The last two months have been hell. I've been keeping my distance but it's been killing me. I watch him when he doesn't see me and I celebrate each time he's made a gain in his motion or weight. I've come early on Tuesdays so that I can see him leave the group room; desperate for the day he tells me he's ready. And now that I'm looking at him—truly and clearly looking at him—I see that he's been waiting just as desperately for me.

"He's not my boyfriend." I smile when the words finally break free.

"You're date?" he asks no relief to be heard in his voice. I shake my head slowly.

"Friend and roommate."

Mateo squeezes my hands tightly and then lets them go. He moves to touch my face, holding me gently as he looks into my eyes. "I missed you even though you've been right in front of me." He makes my stomach flip and my heart beat wildly. "I watch you everyday. I think of your name as I jog and plan where I can take you when you finally agree to a date."

I fist his shirt at his sides and pull him even closer, sucking his lip into my mouth this time and feeling my head spin from the words he's shared. "I've been waiting for you," I say, my throat tightening making the words hoarse and needy.

"Sunshine, I've been right here the whole time."

Part 33

Mateo

She feels so good against me I worry I won't be able to walk out of here. Her hands are clutching my shirt, something I'd help her remove if we weren't in a dark hallway in a dirty dive bar. Her dress is killing me as it is, but now that I've mussed her up, the swell of her tits seems almost obscene and her dress is just inches from showing me the place that will most likely be my undoing. I feel the heat of her on my thigh and it's not until just now that I realize it's my injured leg and I don't care at all that she's touching it.

I slide my hands down her body, so fucking grateful that it doesn't belong to anyone else. My hands slip over her ass and I slide her against my leg just because I know it will driver her crazy before moving my hands lower and pulling the hem of her dress down to make sure she's covered. I want only my eyes on the skin beneath. "This dress is awesome," I say as I look down at her pressed against me. I wish we were back at my place so I could get her out of it because I know it would look even better on my floor. "I don't think I've ever seen you in a dress."

"I don't usually wear them." I didn't think her cheeks could get any more flushed, but they do.

"You've get killer legs, sunshine. And your other parts aren't bad either," I waggle my eyebrows and she giggles. Just like that we're back to how things were before I screwed them up.

"You're not so bad yourself," she replies. "What are you doing later?" I can see her pulse thumping away in her neck. She's anxious and I hate that my answer isn't the one she'll want to hear. I kiss her neck above her pulse.

"My friends are here from out of town. One of them is leaving tonight, but the other two don't get on a plane until tomorrow." I've missed them too, but if I had to choose, I'd want to spend my night with Ashlyn. Only I can't make that choice because they are staying at my place and it would be a total dick move. "What are you doing?" I ask because I want her to tell me she is going home. I want her to lock herself in and not let any other guy see her like this, all hot and ready because of what we've ben doing. I don't have the right to tell her any of that.

"I'm going to play wingman for Rhett. Try and see if he can get the bartender to take him home." The relief hits me hard and I laugh. Thank god I don't have to kill him.

"Don't leave here without me. I've been working on something. I want to make sure you get home safe too." Her eyes look at me curiously, but she nods her head. "I'll walk you back to the bar." I finally step away from her and she adjusts her dress. Then I hold out my hand and she takes it, causing my heart to soar with pride and contentment.

Her friend is sitting on a stool, leaning across the bar to spit game at the young woman behind it. She's clearly loving every minute, tossing her hair around and batting her lashes. He's for sure getting lucky tonight. Me on the other hand, I look over to the table to find my friends all making kissy kissy faces at me and I laugh. I'm not getting lucky tonight, but I've waited a long time to have Ashlyn by my side again and one more night isn't going to kill me.

"Rhett," she says, pulling the man's attention away from the girl behind the bar. "This is..." she doesn't have to finish because he's already holding a hand out to me.

"Mateo. I've heard a lot about you. I'm Rhett." We shake and I'm grateful I didn't come into this swinging because he's actually not a bad guy at all. Ashlyn excuses herself to go to the bathroom for real this time and we both watch her go. Me because I love watching her do anything, and him because he's looking out for her. It makes me wonder why he let us disappear together for so long. "She's a great girl," he says, sitting down again and looking pointedly at the seat beside him until I sit down.

"Yes she is." I'm still watching the hallway, nervous that some other guy is going to try to talk to her and I'll lose my shit.

"She's been unbearable the last few weeks. I don't know what you've done to get her this sprung on you, but whatever it is, you've got her." The bartender pours me my whiskey and then fills up a shot glass for him.

"I'm pretty gone myself," I answer before tossing the red straw and tipping the glass back.

"I saw that. It's the only reason I let you go after her. I don't know why the two of you haven't figured your shit out yet, but I think it would be best for everyone involved if you did it soon." He lifts his glass up in a toast and then takes the shot. I smile, strangely happy that she's been as on edge as I have.

"Thanks for looking out," I tell him as I see Ashlyn emerge from the hallway. "I'll take it from here." He looks me over for a minute and then nods his head.

Extending his hand out to shake mine he says, "If you break her heart—I'll mend it." His words seem innocent, but I know that was the most threatening thing a man could tell another man. I don't hate him for it, and I hope that he won't hate me for never giving him that chance.

Part 34

A shlyn

We're all at the table now, Rhett and I along with Mateo and his two friends. One of them, Lucas, had to leave a few hours ago to catch a flight home to his wife. Listening to him talk about her and eventually show me pictures when it was clear he was getting drunk, was the sweetest thing ever. If I had to bet, I'd bet money those two are going to make it the distance. He is a star worshiping her like the moon.

Rhett is waiting for the bartender to get off work so he can take her home and most likely keep me up all night with the fun they are about to have. I look over at Mateo as he tells a story to Wes, a handsome young guy he calls Lee. I've never seen him this happy and watching makes me smile so big my own cheeks hurt. When the story is over, Mateo settles back down in his chair and puts his hand on my knee. He's been doing it all night, but as the hours have gone on and the alcohol has been drunk, that hand keeps roaming higher and higher and his proximity to my body is getting closer and closer.

"I wish you were coming home with me," he whispers in my ear. The heat of his breath fans out across my shoulder and I practically tremble. His friends are staying the night and I know from being in his place that there would be nowhere private for us to go. I also wouldn't expect him to ditch his friends to come back to my place. They are only in town for tonight and I can see how much he's enjoying their company. About twenty minutes before closing time, I tell him I can't make it any longer. I need to go home and go to bed before all the alcohol of the night makes a return visit all over our table.

"I'm going to ride with her to make sure she makes it ok," he announces to the table, pulling me to his side. "You guys catch a cab back to my place at closing and I'll meet you back there right after. Just leave the door unlocked." He tosses his keys to Liam. All of us are pretty drunk, having spent the last few hours drinking and getting to know each other. I'm not worried about anyone driving because we've all agreed to grab cabs home.

"Are you going to be ok?" I ask Rhett. His cheeks are a light pink, no doubt from the shots he's been taking. He laughs and shrugs his shoulders.

"We're going to find out," he says loudly, making Liam and Wes snort with laughter.

"You should quit now before you disappoint the poor girl," Liam teases. "She's been trying to loosen you up all night. Imagine her getting in your pants just to find out you can't close the deal. Another one down to whiskey dick."

Rhett flips him the bird, but pushes his last shot away. "Hasn't happened yet, but there's a first for everything." He looks at me through bloodshot eyes, "You Ok to go home with him. I'll take you if you would prefer."

I smile and shake my head. "I'm fine. Goodnight everyone!" I say a little too loudly and Mateo laughs as he tucks me beneath his arm to help hold me up as we step back from the table. We walk out of the bar and stand in the cold night air as we wait for the cab to come. Mateo wraps his arms around me, tucking my head beneath his chin as I rest my cheek on his chest. It feels so good to be held by him. Even though I can smell the whiskey on his breath, he still smells like himself and I inhale again, hoping to never miss it like I had these last few months.

"Come on sunshine," he says as he open the cab door for me to get in. I go in first, feeling his eyes on me as I try and fail to get in gracefully. He bites his lip and shakes his head as he climbs in behind me. We are only a few blocks away from my place and I hate that my time with him for tonight is almost over. I want to touch him, but I'm on his right side. I won't make that mistake again.

We ride in silence, but his hand reaches for mine and pulls it across his leg until my palm is flat against his thigh. He's looking out the window, watching lights go by and for a moment everything stands still for me. Time just seems to stop. He might not realize what he's done, but I do. I can feel the bumps beneath my palms and the way his skin feels harder there than just beyond my fingertips. I'm facing him, watching his face and trying not to get emotional about how far he's come.

When we stop for a red light, he turns to me and smiles. He uses his other hand to tuck some of my hair behind my ear and then says, "You really look beautiful tonight sunshine." He kisses me, more tenderly than before and I move my hand to his hair, trying hard to bring him closer. We kiss until we get to the end of my block. When he pulls away suddenly I try to figure out why.

"Stop here," he tells the driver and I try to correct him but he holds a finger up to his lips. He pays the driver and we watch him pull away.

"This isn't where I live," I inform him with a laugh.

"I know. I wanted to walk you home." I stop laughing and look into his eyes. He smiles at me shyly and I love the way it's barely visible from beneath his beard. "I've wanted to do this since that first night you were at my place. I just didn't ever want to hold you back." He takes my hand in his and pulls me towards my place. He has a slight limp, but it doesn't slow us down at all. We don't even talk. I just hold his hand and stay as close to him as possible, at times leaning my head on his shoulder. There are cabs everywhere, dropping off people after the bars have closed but it doesn't take away from this time together. I can't believe how far he's come in such a short time.

"Thank you for tonight," I say when we finally stop in front of my place. I kiss him deeply, holding onto his jaw so I can feel his beard beneath my fingers. His hands find my waist and hold tight, making sure there is not an ounce of space between us. "Do you want to come up?" I ask him hopefully. I know his friends should be back to his place at any moment and that Rhett and the lovely bartender will be here soon too.

"Yes, I definitely want to. Probably more than I've wanted to do anything in my life."

"But..." I say knowing already that one's coming.

"But you're drunk sunshine and so am I." He kisses my lips again but this time it's more chaste. "I've waited two months for you to invite me in," and we both know he isn't talking just about my place. "I want to remember every minute of it." He kisses my shoulder and I close my eyes, tipping my head to give him more access and with the hopes of feeling his rough beard along my neck. "I also want to make sure it's what you really want." His warm, wet lips run up my neck and then back down again. "I want your head to be clear when you give your heart to me."

I open my mouth to tell him that he already has it. It's been his for a long time now, but just as I'm about to say the words a cab pulls up. We step aside as the laughter and noises spill out of the open window. "Were at my place!" Rhett shouts and points at the building. He's completely trashed. It makes me giggle. The bartender opens the door and rolls her eyes. She's trying to seem annoyed, but I can see the small smile on her face.

"Let's get you to bed," she pleads, helping him out of the seat. I might stop her if he didn't tell me earlier not to cockblock him with her tonight. He made me promise no matter how drunk he got, I'd not get in the way of him taking her to bed. I'm not really that worried about it because right now I'd guess that tonight is going to be the first night he might experience some performance issues. The girl doesn't seem to mind. She has that look in her eye that hints at something deeper than a crush.

Rhett hands the cab driver a wad of bills and then waves him off. He wraps his arm around the girl's shoulder, and I'm pretty sure it's more to help him stay up than to guide her to our door. "See you in the morning." He whisper shouts in our direction and both Mateo and I chuckle and give him a wave. We watch them stumble up the stairs and get inside.

"Goodnight sunshine."

"Goodnight Mateo." I get up on my tiptoes and kiss him one last time. He waits and watches to make sure I get inside safe.

Part 35

Mateo

    I find her immediately on Monday morning as I step into the PT office. She's already helping Levi with something I know he could do by himself, but he just looks at me like he snuck a cookie knowing he was going to get caught. Motherfucker. I flip him off with a grin and head over to the mat to stretch. Lying on my back I start by pulling my knee up to my chest. I'm a little tight today and I wonder if it's because I didn't do anything yesterday besides lying around nursing a hangover.

"I'm leaving for a meeting upstairs," Jane says as she stands above me. "If you need anything you can ask Ashlyn." I can't believe she hasn't figured out that there is something between the two of us, but I'm not about to bring any attention to it.

"Ashlyn. Got it." My voice sounds strained as my thigh protests the stretch with a sharp burn like a hot knife in my quad. She walks away, satisfied that she's off the hook and I close my eyes and use some deep breathing to keep from throwing up with the pain.

"It might help if you warm it up a little first," Ashlyn's sweet voice says moving closer to my ear. I open my eyes and find her kneeling beside me, watching my form as I hold my knee.

"I feel like I take one step forward and two back every time I take a day off."

"You had fun. Don't beat yourself up over it. This is going to be your body for the rest of your life. If you let a little regression get to you, you'll want to throw in the towel every few months." Her hand wraps around my ankle and guides my leg so I straighten it out. "I think you just need to relax." Then she makes that impossible by putting both of her hands on the muscle right above my knee.

She positions her thumbs in some magical way that makes them feel like they were design to fit in the groove. With enough pressure to cause some pain, but not enough to make me wince, she pushes up, stretching my quad. Her hands slide up my thigh until her fingers are just about an inch from my groin. I hold my breath and feel myself tense, wanting so badly for her to touch me but knowing that her intention is not the same as mine in this moment.

Letting go, she moves her hands back down to the starting position and repeats the stretch. She's watching her work, "Were those friends from around here?" she asks like she isn't driving me insane with her touch.

"Um," I try to think but my mind is full of too many other thoughts to focus on the answer. I try harder and will myself not to feel her fingers on the inside of my groin. "No."

"You're one friend," she starts to ask, but then stops all movement to try and remember his name. It's torture pure and simple. My brain is screaming in agony at the way she's stopped inching up my leg. "Lucas? Garver?" she's so cute the way she purses her lips and shakes her head until a few wispy strands of hair fall around her face.

"Garver," I answer. She's getting one word. That's all I can manage. I don't even realize what I'm doing until my fingers are sweeping across her forehead and tucking her loose hair behind her ear. She doesn't flinch or pull away, but her eyes jump up to mine bright with desire and wide with the surprise of my hands on her in such a tender way. I slowly move my hand back down to the mat at my side.

Her chest is rising higher now, her cheeks painted that beautiful soft pink. "Garver," she repeats. "Did he make it back ok?"

I don't want to be talking about him right now. I want to be talking about how good her lips look and how incredible it feels for her hands to be wrapped around my thigh. I want her to tell me it's been long enough and this exile from her touch is finally over. Actually, I don't want to be talking about anything. I want to be touching her—holding her. "Yes," I answer quickly.

"So your other friends are still here or...?" she doesn't finish her sentence. Her thumbs are now so high they press against my pelvic bone, her fingers sculpted around my thigh so that I can feel the back of her hand against the part of me that has had enough of this talking and wants more of the touching. The blood in my body is hot and aggressive. It's pumping with all of its force to my dick and there is no image I can begin to think of that's going to change its destination.

Screw puppy dogs and old ladies. My hormones are on a mission and I can practically hear my pulse chanting her name like demanding cadence.

I take a quick glance around the room. Levi is on a machine facing away from us and the other therapist is working with an older vet in the far back. Still, anyone could turn around at any minute or walk through the door and see us here on the floor, her hands so close to my dick it twitches in its attempt to get closer. I'm in tight boxer briefs and an old pair of sweats, but this is going to be hard to shrug off if anyone looks in our direction. With one hand, I adjust myself and with the other, I capture the wrist of her hand nearest to my groin.

Her eyes open a little wider, her breaths coming in short pants as I move her hand and hold it away from my body. I whisper hoarsely, "You're gonna need to move your hands." She looks down at her hands and I see the second she registers what I'm talking about. The light blush turns a few shades darker.

"I'm sorry," she whispers and then takes a quick look around the room. When she sees the coast is all clear, her eyes return to mine and a smile forms in her perfect lips. She wets them innocently, but my body responds as if she's just licked me. I close my eyes and groan quietly.

"Not helping." My words make her giggle. I sit up, moving my legs into a position where my excitement won't be so obvious. She's still laughing as I give her an angry look. I can't keep it on my face very long before I'm laughing too. I few heads finally turn in our direction to see what's so funny, but we just quiet down. I've missed her. Not just how good she can make me feel when her hands are on me, but the way she's like a ray of sunshine that seems to glitter even brighter when she's happy. "Let me take you out tonight?" I ask when everyone has gone back to their exercises.

"I'd like that."

"The doctor cleared me to drive," I say unable to hide how proud that makes me. The feeling only grows more intense when I see that she practically beams with excitement.

"Mateo! That's great!" She throws her arms around my neck and holds me tight. "You worked so hard for that."

I rub my hand up her back, "You're right, I worked really hard." Then I move so that only she can hear my next words, "But driving wasn't what I was working towards." I let her go and stand up, extending a hand down to her so that I can help her to her feet. Her hand feels so right in mine and I tug her up and close, "I'll pick you up at 6, sunshine." I'm not going to tell her what I was working so hard towards, because if everything goes right tonight—I'll show her.

****Hi readers!! We got this story up to #39 in romance. If we can get it to the top 10, I'll write that bonus Dear Bailey chapter. You can help by voting (and making sure you've voted every chapter), commenting (and please, please, please tag your friends in the comments on the chapters so that they can help to), and sharing. Share it on social media or with your followers here on Wattpad. I will do a poll to see what you would want to read more about from Lucas and Bailey. The idea with the most votes will win. Will it be when Lucas and Bailey are back together of the first time after he comes home? Their Honeymoon? Their anniversary?

Part 36

Ashlyn

I'm pacing by the time 6pm rolls around. Rhett is on the couch watching me stalk back and forth while I wait for the doorbell to ring. He lifts his beer up to his mouth and takes a sip as I make another pass. "We're definitely going to lose our deposit. I can't imagine the landlord being cool with the path you are leaving in the carpet." I glare at him, but also check to make sure he's being sarcastic because I known I've done a few laps and it's totally possible I've left matted down carpet in my wake.

"I don't usually get this nervous," I say, shaking out my hands.

"What's there to be nervous about? You guys have already hooked up. It's not like you don't know if he likes you or not." He grabs a small pillow and tosses it at my head. I turn at the perfect moment and it bounces off my forehead. We both laugh and then I scoop it up and whiz it back in his direction. "Easy. I'm trying to help and you're trying to take my head off.

"It's like I'm all bottled up. It makes me want to crawl out of my skin." I turn and head back towards the front door. When the doorbell rings I startle.

I hear Rhett say under his breath, "I'm sure he's eager to help you out with that." I roll my eyes even though he can't see me. Rhett and I had been in a relationship for a year when we were in the crash. We fell apart trying to heal ourselves and when the dust had settled, we just weren't the same people that had gotten into that car. It took a while to find each other as friends again, but we pulled through. I'm amazed at how far we've come. It doesn't hurt me to see him bring girls home anymore, and he's never been bothered by anyone I've brought around. Then again, I haven't really brought anyone around. Usually I make sure to spend my time with men outside this apartment. Our worlds colliding at the bar was an accident.

"You alright?" I ask him over my shoulder with my hand on the knob. I need things to be good between us. I need to know he's OK with me dating someone else in front of him. It's the first time we've been at this crossroads.

"Cheese and crackers, open the bloody door." He flicks his hand in my direction and then stands so he can leave the room.

"Rhett," I start, but he doesn't let me finish.

"It stings. It's hard to see you with someone else."

"You know I've seen other men," I protest.

"They didn't hurt." He shrugs one shoulder and then looks away before returning his eyes to mine. "You didn't care about them." He points to the door as if he can see through it. "You care about HIM."

"I...."

"Just open the door and let him in, Ash." He looks defeated, but not angry. I wait another second, debating what would be the best move for our friendship and what that might mean for Mateo and I. I stare at Rhett, but my hand turns the knob because while I love Rhett dearly, I'm not in love with him anymore. His lip pinch together and he gives me a small nod before turning and heading for his bedroom without another word.

"Hi, sunshine." Mateo stands on my porch, a bouquet of fresh sunflowers in his hand.

"Hi." I say as he hands them to me. He got a hair cut, but he kept his beard. It's trimmed and I realize that I would be disappointed if he had shaved it for tonight. It's a part of him that I've grown to love. "I'll just put these in some water. Come inside." I open the door wider and motion for him to enter. He looks down the hall just as I hear Rhett's door close. The sound is crisp and carries down the hall, standing out against the quiet of the living room. Mateo looks at me as if he could tell something big just happened and all I can do is shrug my shoulders. I don't know how to tell him that the door being closed down the hall is a physical representation of Rhett emotionally shutting me out.

Part 37

M ateo

It feels as cold as ice in here, but the temperature is fine. Ashlyn looks through the cupboards but I can tell she isn't really paying attention to what she's trying to find. Something is off and I have a feeling it has more to do with the closed door at the end of the hall than it does with her quest to find a vase. I move behind her, leaning against the kitchen island and watching her open and close the cupboards mindlessly. She looks like she might cry and now I feel that protect instinct start to come to life inside my heart.

She stands with her back to me, staring into the cupboard in front of us. Her little blue dress rides up her perfect thighs and barely covers the bottom of her ass. She looks beautiful just like I knew she would. It's such a stunning sight and I can't stop watching her move around, even if I know she's accomplishing nothing. Finally, I step up behind her and put my hands on her shoulders. She freezes at my touch and lets out a breath she's been holding.

"Ashlyn," I say softly, running my hands down her arms until she lowers them from the cupboard handles. I hold her at her biceps, squeezing just enough to get her attention. "What just happened?" I spin her around so that I can look her in the eyes. There is so much going on behind them, but she doesn't speak. "I get the feeling you aren't going to find what you need in this kitchen." She looks down at our feet, but I slide my hands down her arms until I'm holding her hands. "Tell me what happened."

Her hair is curled and she's pulled a section of it back with a small clip. She smells like apples again and something sweeter. The gloss on her lips shines as she pulls the lower between her teeth, worrying it as she thinks about her answer. "It's a long story," she says and I know she's just trying to get out of sharing it.

"I've got all night." She doesn't know me very well yet, or she would know that I'm a persistent guy. I'm getting this answer even if I have to pry it out of her like a dentist removing a bad tooth. Once it out, she'll feel much better.

She looks in the direction of the hallway and confirms my theory that Rhett has something to do with it. If she'd just spit it out, I could get on to the beating his ass part of the evening. I must move, even if I don't realize I'm doing it, because she squeezes my hands and tugs them back to her. "I'll explain it all at dinner." I look from her resolved expression to the hallway and back. Trying to decide if I really need the whole backstory or if her being upset is reason enough to go find him.

I've been turning his words to me at the bar over and over in my head. I thought he was just being a protective friend at the time, but his threat to mend her heart has begun to burn a hole in my stomach and leave a sour taste on my tongue. Truth be told, I don't want any other man near her heart to begin with. If he wants a shot at it, he's going to have to pry it from my fingers because once she gives it to me I'm keeping it forever. "Dinner is a long way away from that door at the end of the hall," I reply, not really bothering to hide my unspoken promise of doing something to her roommate if the story reveals an action by him that I don't agree with.

"That's why it's best to tell it somewhere else." She releases one of my hands and lifts up to kiss my cheek. "Come on. Let's get out of here." She tugs on my arm and leads me out of the kitchen back to the living room. She won't even look down the hall now and my gut is churning with dread and curiosity. I have a feeling I'm not going to like what she's working herself up to sharing. She tucks a clutch purse beneath her arm and opens the front door, inviting me to step outside.

I look at her for a moment wanting to insist I be told right now, but she really doesn't owe me anything. I take a few steps so that I'm standing so close the toes of our shoes are touching. I lift her chin with my fingers so that I can see her eyes which are filled with sadness instead of her usual bright happiness, "You look absolutely beautiful tonight, but someone has stolen your shine." I lean in and brush my lips against hers because I can't wait another minute. "I won't stop until I get it back." I guide her chin a little closer until her lips part and invite me in.

Part 38

A shlyn

The waiter leaves our table and instantly Mateo's eyes are on mine. He's waited patiently for me to explain the freeze out by Rhett. He folds his hand and leans in as I clear my throat and try to think of where I should even start. "So we were seniors in high school. Rhett and I had started dating in the middle of our junior year." I can see the tension in Mateo's jaw as he listens. "We were friends first. I actually hung out with a big group of boys in school and he was part of that group. We were the closest out of the group. Actually, the two of us and Joseph." I feel my throat tighten at the mention of his name. It usually doesn't move me to tears anymore, but something about sharing it with Mateo makes it burn all over again.

"Rhett and started dating in the middle of our junior year. It was a really slow build that started with us just talking more, then us hanging out outside the group and then somewhere around the sixth month we told everyone and made it official. I didn't know that Joseph liked me too and that it would be hard on their friendship. Rhett felt bad that he knew about Joseph liking me and still pursued our relationship. I think that's why everything feels like it was in slow motion."

Mateo adjusts his potion, waiting from me to continue.

I laugh softly without humor, "We, um, we hadn't really done much more than kissing. My dad is a minister," I smile at the thought and his shoulders seem to relax with the information. "We were going shopping for prom. It was finally starting to feel normal again—you know, not so much tension between Rhett and Joseph. It was awful for a while. I hated that our relationship was breaking up their friendship, but Rhett...it just ate him up." I fight to keep the emotion out of my voice. "He couldn't talk to his best friend about his time with me, and Joseph wouldn't hang out with the group, if the two of us were going to be there together."

Mateo nods his head, telling me he's still right there, patiently listening as I share the toughest moment of my life. "We had just gone to get them fitted for tuxes. It was the first time the three of us had done anything alone since the big announcement. Rhett and Joseph had gotten into an argument because Joe was honest and told him it would be hard to watch us be together that night." I tuck my hair behind my ears and cross my arms. "An elderly man had a heart attack while driving. He was unconscious when he hit our stopped car with his foot on the accelerator. We flipped and were crushed between the metal of our car and his."

"I'm sorry," he says quietly and I can hear the sincerity in his voice. I nod my head and pull in a breath so he can hear the rest.

"Rhett lost his leg, but Joe lost his life. We tried to make it work for a while, but the rehab we both had to do for our injuries was just too much. I don't think Rhett really ever got over how things had been in the minutes before Joe died." I feel so much lighter with that off my chest, but I know that doesn't explain the way Rhett had acted.

"What was it like to walk away from that accident?" I've never really been asked that question and it takes a minute for me to think about the answer.

"I was in physical therapy for a year. I missed my senior year events, but I wouldn't have been up for them anyway. There was this gray cloud that loomed over me for a few years. I had to do some therapy to get past it."

"Is that why you chose to become a physical therapist?" he asks.

"I had nothing but time in between appointments. I finished my senior year quickly and started right away on college. I was worried if I didn't keep going I'd fall apart."

"And Rhett?"

"He just fell apart." I'm hit with a memory of him trying to climb the cemetery hill with his new prosthetic. It makes my heart twist and throb. "He stopped talking to all of us for a while. Then he got into some trouble with his pain medication. As you know, it would be so easy to take them for the pain in your heart when they're really prescribed for your leg." He's already nodding his head. He pulls his hands up until they are steeped in front of him.

"So what does that mean for the two of you?" I expected anger, but it's a question without judgment. I'm speechless for a minute and he moves to fill in the quiet between us. "I know what it's like to have regrets with a friend. I know what it's like to live when they didn't. It's as debilitating as it is consuming. You push people away when you really need them close."

"It could never be the way it was," I answer honestly. "There's been too much time to get back to when it worked. I'm a different person. He's a different person."

"But he still loves you." It isn't a question.

"Maybe. Yes. I will always love him too, for what we've been through, for how we had to help each other climb out of it literally as well as mentally. I guess he didn't realize there was still something more there for him until you came along." The waiter brings our water as we stay still, waiting for him to leave so we can talk again.

"What do I have to do with it? He's reminded because of my injury?" His hand moves almost unconsciously to his thigh.

"No. I image it's because he's seen the way I look in love...only this time I'm not looking at him."

Part 39

M ateo

The toughest part of my recovery has not been from the wounds to my leg. It's been the battle my mind has been waging with itself. In the beginning it was flashbacks—my experience loading the stapler today while being transported to filling my magazine in a place far away, but never forgotten. From the ashes of this battle came a fierce hyper-vigilance that left me tense and drained of my energy. When I learned to distinguish what was happening in real-time from what was happening in the recesses of my memory, a new battle emerged. The grief of what I've lost—who I've lost—fought along side an abundance of crippling guilt and anxiety against my soul's need to be healed. I'm convinced there will never be a clear victor in that campaign.

Now that I'm almost a year out of my trauma, I fully grasp that the conflict should be over. Sometimes I feel I've won and sometimes I know I have not, because even in victory there was a price to be paid. I'm a veteran of war returning home, picking up my pieces and trying to make a life with them. So when Ashlyn's words fill the space between us, I have to take a minute to run them through all the mental filters I've created. I need to check for validity and then examine the present to make sure they don't speak of something in the past.

She's here right now, sitting in front of me, the girl who has no idea how important she's been in my recovery. Not just for what she's done directly by helping my stretches and pushing my limits, but by how she found within me the parts of my character that I was sure had spilled from my body like the blood from my wound—persistence and motivation. I got better not just for her, but also because of her.

I feel the emotion clogging my throat, the joy of what she's just confessed hitting my heart like pure adrenaline. I've known for a while now that she is my one. The one woman I'd compare all others to, the one who seemed to know me better than I've ever known myself, and the one who I'd never get over if she walked away. I just had never imagined that I'd be worthy of her. I don't mean in that sappy way that men tease about how women are naturally better and men are forever unworthy. I mean it with sincerity. Ashlyn is sunshine and perseverance personified and even on my best day, I couldn't come close to making the impact she does on the people around her. And yet, with my war-torn body and battle weary mind, she still chooses me.

"I'll never let you regret it," I tell her, my voice raspy as it pushes out past the knot in my heart and lump in my throat. Her head tilts in question and I realize that she's just told me of this horrible crash and the loss of a friend and I'm speaking in a conversation in my head she hasn't really been I apart of. I smile, "I'll never let you regret loving me," I clarify. "I won't give you the chance," I say with conviction. "Monday through Sunday, twenty-four seven, through every glorious good time and of course all of the bad—I'm going to love you like you're the sun in my sky. Every part of me will revolve around you because I'm certain that's the way God intended."

The waiter approaches with our dinner, but Ashlyn keeps her eyes one me. Joy is a beautiful emotion. The way her cheeks lift and her lips curl, the melodic sound that floats from her mouth as she chuckles. Relief is a worthy contender, the soft sigh on her lips and the way her shoulders relax. But neither emotion can hold a candle to acceptance. It doesn't matter what her shoulders are doing, or the way her lips move—I'm only watching her eyes. They say without words that she trusts me and that all the outside shit in our lives—the big staircases and stiff muscles, the bad dreams and torn flesh—none of it matters because it can't stop what we have. Nothing can stop forever, and if anyone can conquer future downfalls and setbacks it's us. We've already learned to walk again thus proving that nothing can hold us back.

"I don't need your life to revolve around mine," she says after the waiter has left us alone again. "I just want someone to walk beside me."

I know this is serious and I shouldn't tease, but that's just not who I am with her. "Even if my limp might slow us down?" I lean in a little closer and take her hand.

"What can I say?" she asks with a small shrug of her shoulder and a smile that makes my heart explode, "You're sexy walk kind of does it for me."

A laugh bubbles up from my chest and I squeeze her hand in mine. "Should I make a quick lap around this place to make sure you'll want to let me take you home?" I feign being curious, using my fist and thumb to point over my shoulder in the direction I'd leave so she could watch. This time, she tugs my hand and pulls me closer, leaning over the table and kissing my lips as she giggles.

"Honey, you sealed that deal when you bought me flowers." And that right there is the reason I'm going to love her for the rest of my life.

Part 40

A shlyn

He's gotten remarkably better and climbing his stairs. He holds my hand and walks beside me, never once slowing me down. I feel proud of him and proud to be with him, both filling my heart so full it feels three sizes too big for my chest. He unlocks the door and waits for me to step past him to come inside. Things look the same as they had last time, but there are a few differences.

His table is clear of any papers he had around his laptop. All that sits there is a brown large envelope like you'd get from a printing store, and a laptop that isn't plugged in or even turned on. I can't help but hope he hasn't given up writing because I just wouldn't be able to stand that news. I think everyone has a story to tell, but some people were meant to share that story with the masses. Mateo is one of those people.

I also notice a few pictures framed and resting on the various counters and furniture. Before, his apartment had given away nothing about his friendship or family. Now I feel like there are little keys, opening invisible doors to the branches of his life tree. There is an older couple in one on the kitchen counter, a little girl running through a grassy field in another and my favorite—a picture of Mateo in uniform with three other sharply dressed Marines.

"He must be Pines," I say, running my finger over the only man in the picture I didn't recognize from the bar.

His smile is sad, but not in the way that makes my throat tighten with the weight of it. It's more a reminiscent sort of feeling, like he misses his friend, but still appreciates the experience of having known him. I know that feeling very well. I have my own corner in my heart that holds a piece of who I lost. My hand rubs across my heart as I study their faces. They look young and yet still so courageous.

"That was taken at the airport before we deployed." He lifts the frame from the counter and holds it closer so he can see his friends' faces. "It feels like a lifetime ago some days, but others I would swear I just got home." He sets it back down and takes my hand. "I told you I've been working on towards something." We move over to the couch and he guides me to sit down. His smile is child-like and makes my own lips curl.

"I think I like where this is going," I tease, but he doesn't sit down with me yet. He walks over to the small table and retrieves the brown envelope near his computer.

"I like your thinking, but there is something I want to show you first."

"That's what she said," I can't help myself. We both laugh and he shakes his head and waggles a finger at me like a mother would when scolding a child.

"You're worse than my guy friends." He sits down next to me and I don't fail to notice how much easier that move is for him. He still falls onto the cushion a little abruptly, but overall it is a huge improvement.

"What's that?" I ask as he looks down at the envelope.

"When I didn't have you to keep me busy, I stumbled a bit, literally and figuratively. I wasn't sure what to do with myself if I wasn't looking forward to hanging out. I decided if I couldn't work on winning you over, I needed to work on something I could be proud of. I needed an exit plan for when I've finally reached all of my goals at PT." His hand slides across the paper and he unwraps the string that holds the flap together. My mind races with all the possibilities. Are those loan docs for a home far away? Is it a contract for civilian work on a base in another state? Is it anything that will pull him out of my life when I finally just got him back into it?

"Are you trying to kill me with the suspense?" I ask as I place my hand on top of his over the envelope.

"No," he says, shaking his head to reinforce the word. "I'm trying to take care of us."

Part 41

Mateo

My hand actually shakes a little as I pull the thick stack of crisp white copy paper from the envelope. She won't be the first person to see this, or even the second or third. No, many people have read these words over the last month. They have been examined and judged, discussed and then decided on. I had to learn to let them go so that I could take the first big step into my new life. Maybe that doesn't seem so big to people who take thousands of steps everyday on their perfectly healthy legs, but I know the value of each painstaking step. The hours of therapy that can go into such a move so easily taken for granted by others.

I look up into her eyes as she stares back at mine. Without another word, I hand her the stack and finally feel the anticipation and fear leave my body when the weight of those papers are lifted from my grasp. She slides them onto her lap, her hand fanning out across the top sheet. In the center of the page, my first novel's title stands our boldly in black ink against the white background. It's followed by my full name in subscript.

Ashlyn gasps when she realizes what I've just handed her and she looks back at me, all wide-eyed and full of wonder. "You did it?" she asks. I nod my head and try not to smile too widely. "Oh my God." She looks back down at the stack of paper and grips it in her hands like feeling the pages beneath her skin will make it more real. I chuckle, I did the exact same thing with the worker at the print shop had handed it to me. I know she wants to flip to the first page, but she hesitates out of respect for my privacy.

"It's so thick it barely fits in my hand," she whispers and I can't miss this chance to get her back.

"That's what she said," I say in my best frat-boy voice. She tips her head back as she laughs and I know nothing else in the world will ever make me feel happier than having something to do with that. She punches me lightly on my arm and then returns her attention to that first page. I nudge her with my shoulder and when her eyes look up at me this time I worry she might be about to cry. "Turn the first page," I tell her.

"Really? Are you sure?" She looks back and forth from the pages to my face.

"Well my plan wasn't for you to just hold it."

In unison we both finish, "That's what she said."

Her fingers lightly lift the title page and beneath it she finds the dedication. It was always going to be her. Even before I knew her, the universe had put into play the plan to get us together and the page had remained blank until I figured out that it was her name that should grace it.

To my sunshine, my only sunshine-

This started out for me,

became about you,

and was finished for us.

I could put a million words on paper but they will never do for you what your light has done for me. I love you.

Part 42

Ashlyn

I want to read further. I want to dive into the story that has filled his time while I've been at home with thoughts consumed by his recovery and what could be. Instead I fling my arms around his neck, pulling him to me for a kiss that I've been waiting for all night. His hand finds it's way into my hair like he needs to be able to hold me even when something so important is still between us. I pull back and set it aside on the table so I can touch his lips again.

"Aren't you going to wait..." he can't finish before I kiss him. I close my eyes because our faces are so close together I can see nothing with them open. My hands are on his face, trailing along his beard—the scruffy part of him I've missed so much. Our pace is quick at first, grabbing for each other and holding on to whatever we can so that our bodies won't fall apart.

"I love you," I say when he pulls away to catch his breath, but that only makes him come back for more. I giggle as he smiles against my mouth, kissing and seeking the connection that has been so close before and yet so far away in the big picture.

"I love you," he confesses as if he hasn't already put it in writing. His hand moves up to my jaw, trailing softly as his mouth meets mine over and over again. His warm palm cups my neck, his thumb caressing my cheek until my insides are melted like the chocolate in a hot cookie. I kick off my heels and move to kneel on the couch, and he toes off his shoes and takes his socks off quickly, watching as I rise up on my knees to lift my dress over my head. His eyes take me in, wandering over every inch of my exposed skin, but always finding my own gaze as if he can't decide if he wants to look at my skin or my soul.

He pulls his shirt off and tosses it to the side and I kiss his neck, loving the slow swallow of his throat as his skin heats beneath my mouth. "God, Ashlyn," he whispers. I tuck my hand into the waist of his paints and unbutton them, sliding down the zipper with his help as he moves up onto his knees as well. He pushes them down and kicks them off and we are left just inches from each other and only a few items of clothing away from being totally bare.

I hook my thumbs into the lacey waistband of my panties and feel my teeth dig into my bottom lip as I watch his eyes grow heavy with lust and his cheeks warm and pink with the flush of desire. Next I unsnap my bra and toss it somewhere near his shirt on the growing pile of clothing on his floor.

I can see the bulge in his boxers showing me just how much he likes seeing me bare to him, but I hesitate to reach out even when it is all I can seem to think about. I want to feel him touch me and I want my hands all over him. I want to know what each inch of his flesh feels like beneath my fingers and palms. I want so many things with this man, but I know that he has to show me it all in his time.

His thumbs dip beneath the black elastic waist of his boxers and he keeps my gaze as he slips them down, slowly and at an exquisitely torturous pace. When I see the first peek of smooth skin as his scar begins to appear, I look up to his face, needing him to know if he isn't ready for this yet I can wait. But he just lifts one eyebrow and the stares down at his boxers and then back as if to silently tease me for not watching the show. I smile and return my eyes to right where they want to be. When he pushes them down the length of his thighs and stands to remove them completely, I'm not sure I'll be able to get past how unexpected his courage is and how proud I am of him for overcoming something so difficult.

When we are both naked, he reaches out and touches my face softly, moving slowly into the space between is and holding me at my cheek and waist. His kisses slow down now, but the intensity of all the feelings and every physical sensation feels amplified when the mood switches from lust to love.

He lays me back gently, stretching his long, muscular body above me and settling in between my legs. He doesn't seem in a rush to push inside; instead he pulls back and looks at my face, raining small kisses on my lips and neck as he brushes the hair from my forehead. My legs spread wider so that I can feel more of his body on mine. It's a weight that feels secure and grounding. I link my arm around his neck and close my eyes, loving it when he kisses a trail down my neck and up the other side until he reaches my ear and attests, "I really, really love you." And I fall deeper in love with each syllable he speaks.

Part 43

M ateo

"I love you, more," my sunshine says as I stare down at her, torn between looking at her face and tasting her skin on my tongue. My hand slides along her side and around her ass, lifting and guiding it higher at my hip and then tucking it over my thigh so I'm cradled between her legs. With that side obedient, I return my elbow to the side of her head and start the same coaxing with my other hand along her other side. Finally happy with how tight her legs squeeze around me, I drop a kiss to her nose and then forehead.

"Are you sure this is what you want?" My heart hammers in my chest and my libido begs her silently to say yes. At the same time, my stomach flips, the knowledge that it's been so long since I've been with a girl. I'm not even sure if my leg is going to hold out or if I'll be able to keep up a pleasurable rhythm. I'll never know if I don't try to push myself.

She nods her head and lifts her chin so our lips can meet. Her hands move into my hair and she rolls her hips, stealing my breath in a sharp wave of pleasure as her warm, wet body slides along my hard length. I pull my hips back bracing myself on my elbows at her side. Her hand slips between us and I feel my breath stutter as she grips me, guiding me to her entrance as she looks into my eyes. I move with her, praying my thigh will cooperate tonight so that I can enjoy her and the idea of us.

I close my eyes and tip my head back as I slide in, overwhelmed with the sensation and unable to do anything but focus on the way pre ecstasy races up my spine. Tiny bumps pebble across my skin, pulling everything tight and making it all so achy with the need to find release. I bring my eyes back to her. Her breath pushes out in perfect timing, catching as I begin to draw back. I feel her fingers dig into my skin, her hands beginning to pull at my hair as her own head tips back with the slight arch of her back. Her smooth neck is exposed to me and instinctively I lick it and suck the thin skin into my eager mouth. I won't leave a mark, but I want to.

Her hips rise as soon as I'm pushing forward again, her heels digging into my calves as she presses her hot flesh against me. It's heaven, I'm sure of it. "Mateo." My name on her lips only tightens the ache more—pushing the need to let everything go up to the surface. I roll into her again and again, feeling my own fingers digging for purchase into the cushion of the couch. My heart thuds almost violently in my chest, making my heat grow dizzy and sweat begin to gather along my forehead and down my back. Now we slide along each other's skin—nature working perfectly to create the best movement.

"Hurry," she demands, trying hard to open her eyes, but failing. Her mouth is open to allow the shallow inhale and exhale of breath as I work over her. I don't feel any pain—can't focus on anything but getting her there so I can watch her fall apart from my position above. I press my knees further into the couch so I can thrust quicker and I feel her body tense with her raising climax. I want to swallow it down, breathe it in, and feel every ripple of her muscles so I don't stop. I move quicker and thrust deeper, trying so hard to hold my own orgasm back as she gasps and then moans my name as her body clenches tightly around mine. That's all it takes to send me over the edge with such force I worry I might lose consciousness.

Part 44

Ashlyn

The room is dark as we lay in his bed. We moved here after our time on the couch, when we finally caught our breaths and were able to chase the dizziness from our minds as our hearts slowed their rhythm. Mateo told me about his literary agent and how she got him an amazing publishing deal. And when we got to his room he pulled back his covers and climbed beneath them, holding his arm open as an invitation for me to lie on his chest. I didn't even hesitate.

Tomorrow there will be more challenges. Some will be small like a pulled muscle or a tall flight of stairs on an icy morning, and other will seem insurmountable. Maybe the memories of our traumas will come back for a visit or fate will decide we'd escaped its' angry grasp unjustly and throw us another trauma to overcome. I don't know how to prepare for all the what ifs, but I know that I won't be alone when they appear before me.

Recovering from something heartbreaking is a life long experience. You never get to check the box that says it's no longer a part of who you are. It will always be there like a marker in your DNA, but how much power you give it is up to you. Mateo has chosen to look his heartbreak in the eye everyday. He told me to get to the place he is now, he forced himself to wake up each morning and look at his new body. When he took away the ability for his injury to snatch his confidence, he was able to accept that his scars aren't just reminders of what he's lost, but they're reminders of what he had. Time. The time he had with Pines, and the time he was left with when death didn't take him that day.

As for me, I choose happiness. I conquer my trauma by living in the present. I don't go back to try and make the same mistake twice. So while Rhett will always be important to me, the truth is I knew from the moment he couldn't look at me as we waited to be cut free from his mangled car, that we would never be the same. Too many dreams were crushed in the accident and fences that needed to be mended with Joseph so that we could be secure in our lives together, were left forever broken.

Mateo's arm pulls me closer and I rest my cheek against his strong chest and close my tired eyes. His lips press to the top of my head and he runs his hand down my back as I feel myself drift off to sleep.

Part 45

Mateo

I remember the way it felt when the bullets hit my leg. I remember the sound they made as they tore through my flesh and then my muscle until finally hitting the bone. I remember the weight of Pines as his head rested on my wounded thigh and he took his last breath. I watched the life leave his eyes and heard the slow exhale as all the air left his lungs for the last time. And then I remember the warmth of the blood—his and mine—as it began to seep from our bodies. It mixed together like a metaphor for the brotherhood we weren't given by birth, but we had earned in our time together as Marines. Until a few hours ago I believed it would be the only weight I'd ever remember and the last touch I'd be able to tolerate there. But now I know that I was wrong.

Ashlyn's breaths even out as she falls asleep and I hold her to me. I love the feel of her soft cheek against my chest, her smooth palm resting on my abdomen. I feel the slight tickle of her hair as it fans out across my shoulder and the amusing chill of her cold feet tangled with my own. But of all the places her body meets mine...the warm, healing weight of her thigh resting over my own is my favorite. Tonight I'll let her sleep, because in the morning I plan on doing whatever it takes to make this our new forever.

Ingram Content Group UK Ltd.
Milton Keynes UK
UKHW020626210623
423802UK00010B/31